PAPER DOLLS

CORY TOTH

WARNER HOUSE

PUBLISHING COMPANY

1

It was 2:13 AM when Sherriff Kenneth Reynolds was lazily cruising in his patrol car on a remote section of Route Six, blinking heavily to stay awake. He forced his eyes to readjust as they unintentionally focused on the bugs illuminated for a split second before being swept over the car and back into the night. He was hypnotized by the road passing underneath within the narrow view of his headlights on the choppy road. It was the dead of night and it was unusually dark out, with the moon overshadowed by overcast clouds that swallowed it like dark velvet curtains. A few potholes jarred him and roused his senses, but only for a moment. He had to shake himself awake periodically despite the hot coffee that warmed him and surged his heart in an effort to jumpstart his system.

Reynolds hated working the graveyard shift, but it had been Halloween the evening before, and they needed every man they had out patrolling. The older teenagers, who had been left behind by the magic and fun of Halloween, now had nothing better to do than vandalize other people's property and get themselves into trouble. *Pathetic,* Reynolds thought; all part of growing up, rebelling against the glory and magic of youth no longer theirs, still hopelessly clinging to the excitement of the holiday they had outgrown.

As Reynolds pressed harder on the accelerator pedal, he deeply inhaled the familiar stench of rotten eggs and chemicals produced by the paper mill, the primary source of employment for eighty percent of Victory Falls' residents. Toxic fumes wafted through the air and filled every space within the town, creeping into its citizens' homes and infiltrating their nurseries. The mill's odorous poison was the first breath newborn babies would take and the last they would smell when they died old, worn-out and exhausted after donating their lives to manufacturing paper products. Long after they died, the mill's smokestacks would continue to puff out clouds of pollutants as it gradually burned its workers' lives for fuel.

Reynolds stewed over his coffee, which boiled his blood as his mind unavoidably drifted to the divorce his wife had just asked for. He had received the papers the day before and tried not to think about it because it only made him angry and depressed. *I have never hated anyone more in my life*, was the sentiment that echoed in his mind with more intensity and hate every time he thought it, making his blood pressure spike and his heart pound like a sledgehammer. The stress he was causing himself would surely be the death of him, or, at the very least, would cost him more hair off his head, but he didn't care. He was too damaged to restrain the demons within; thus, they ran amuck through his mind—and there wasn't much keeping them in check when he was alone in a car on a dark back road in the middle of nowhere.

In mid-sip of his coffee, he suddenly gasped and inhaled a gulp of scalding liquid. His body sprang into action and his foot stomped onto the brake pedal. His cruiser rocked forward and screeched to a stop in the middle of the road.

There was a flash of something unexpected ahead of him.

Reynolds spewed out the hot coffee he had inhaled directly into his lungs with an awful choking sound, spraying it all over the dashboard of his patrol car and radio in a fine mist. He repeatedly coughed as he struggled to get control of himself and determine what he had almost hit.

He peered through the speckles of liquid that now covered the windshield and filtered his view. He wiped his shirtsleeve across his mouth, which hung agape in astonishment. There was a small figure in front of his car facing away from him. It was moving. It looked like a young boy walking slowly down the road in the dark, wearing something unusual that confused Reynolds' senses for a moment. He then realized it was a costume—what looked like a Yankees uniform—on the figure, who did not acknowledge the cruiser almost hitting him, the screeching tires or the headlights illuminating him in the pitch-black night.

Reynolds brushed the coffee off his uniform and watched in shock as the boy continued walking away from the patrol car down the middle of the road so far from civilization.

Reynolds was familiar enough with this stretch of road to know that there were no houses for at least a mile. He flicked on his spotlight and pivoted it on its hinge to more clearly illuminate the boy, placing him directly in the light beam. The boy turned, briefly, and looked back at the brilliant light illuminating him, but then continued on his way as though distracted but not deterred.

Reynolds finally took his heavy foot off the brake, which it held pinned to the floor, and edged his patrol car up on the boy with his curiosity growing by the second. He had grown accustomed to expecting the unexpected and every day being different, but this was one of the strangest sights he had encountered. Since there was nothing around but woods and fields, this boy's direction would take him nowhere. It would be at least a two-mile walk to the next town over, Tannersville, and he couldn't remember seeing any houses along that stretch of road before town.

The boy watched the patrol car creep up on him out of the corner of his eye and could feel the heat from the engine on his bare right arm. The spotlight made him squint and he put a hand up to block the painful light. He tried to ignore it; hopeful it would go away and leave him alone.

Reynolds leaned his head out the window. "Hey," he called the boy from behind the spotlight.

The boy tried to see who had called him but couldn't look in the direction of the light. His eyes had adjusted to the dark, and his pupils were dilated, making the bright light painful.

"Hey, kid," the deep voice called again, "I'm talking to you."

The boy stopped walking and stood in the road, still holding a hand up to shield his eyes, trying his best to see past the spotlight.

"Just where on Earth do you think you're walking to?" Reynolds said to him in a fatherly tone, disciplinary but not overly intimidating. He didn't want to scare him away.

The boy put up his other hand to block the light being shined at him. He peered through his fingers at the light aimed at him as though it was an alien spacecraft descended from outer space, fearful but intrigued at the same time.

"How did you even get out here?" Reynolds asked in a friendly tone and waited for the boy to answer, but the boy looked clearly confused, totally lost and hopeless. "Where did you come from, son?" Seeing the boy covering his face with his palms, Reynolds reached up and swiveled the spotlight out of his face, now confident that he intended no harm. He was still in his Halloween costume from the night before. He must have somehow become separated from his group of friends and wandered all the way out here, having totally lost his bearings. "You can talk to me, you know," Reynolds said in a kinder tone to avoid spooking the boy, who clearly had been through some traumatic ordeal that night. "I'm a police officer. It's my job to help people." He could see the boy lower his hands from his face as he looked at the police cruiser and the officer behind the wheel with an expression of bewilderment, as if he had suddenly awoken from sleepwalking and found himself not only outdoors, but in the middle of nowhere being questioned by a stranger.

"Where am I?" the boy finally asked in a quivering voice, staring at the tired looking man behind the wheel of the car.

"You're smack dab in the middle of County Route Six," Reynolds said. "You're lucky you didn't get hit by a tractor trailer, walking out in the road like that. I almost plowed right into you. Now, do you want to tell me exactly what you're doing here?"

The boy paused, clearly disturbed by his lack of ability to answer this question. He looked up the road, in the direction he had been heading, and then back in the direction from which he had come. "I don't know," he answered in a meek voice filled with anxiety and exhaustion.

"Do you live around here?" Reynolds asked, sensing his fear and doing his best not to intimidate the boy.

"I don't know," the boy said, shaking his head at these invasive questions. "I don't know where I am and I don't recognize anything." Judging by his voice and appearance, Reynolds placed him between ten and twelve years old.

"Okay," Reynolds said hesitantly, still unsure of exactly what to make of this as he unbuckled his seatbelt and opened his door.

The boy suddenly backed away from him as he neared, as though he feared being attacked.

"Whoa, easy, there," Reynolds calmed him with his hands in the air, fearing he would turn and run. "I just want to get you home—wherever that may be. I'm trying to help you. If you get in the cruiser with me, I'll take you home," he reasoned with him. "You're not in any sort of trouble or anything."

The boy seemed to calm down. He stopped backing away and appeared willing to accept Reynolds' help.

"Do you know what your address is?" Reynolds asked, hoping he was old enough to know it.

The boy nodded subtly. "Sixteen Maple Terrace," he said slowly in a shaky voice, the address where he had lived his entire life and had memorized since he was four.

"Hop on in, son," Reynolds said with a sweeping motion of his arm and opened the back door of his cruiser. "Sixteen Maple Terrace, it is," he said like a New York City cab driver. "Victory Falls, right? It's right off of Main Street?"

The boy nodded as he lowered himself in slow motion down into the back seat of the cruiser.

"Watch your leg," Reynolds warned as he gently closed the door. Reynolds settled into the driver's seat of the cruiser and closed the door, shifting his weight around to get comfortable, making the vehicle jiggle. "What's your name, son?"

"Landon," he answered plainly, "Landon Daniels."

"Can you tell me why you were wandering out here in the middle of nowhere? Were you in some sort of accident? Did something happen to you?"

"I don't think so." The boy heard a static female voice from the radio on the dashboard, and then a male voice responding a moment later. Looking at the cop through the metal bars that crossed behind the two front seats made him feel like a criminal. The seat of plush tan leather absorbed his weary body like a giant pillow. He took a deep breath and let his muscles relax, realizing how tense they had been. Before he realized how tired he was, he had fallen asleep.

Landon woke up in a groggy state squinting at a bright light again, realizing he was standing before the front door of a house. He was exhausted and just wanted to be left alone. He didn't understand what they were doing on this front porch or what they were waiting for. He looked around at the light above him and was repulsed by the moths and various other flying insects swarming to the light from the darkness, obsessing with it and hurling themselves against the glass of the overhead lantern. They were only a couple feet from his face, and he hoped they didn't fly down at him. His eyes slowly moved down to the dark green front door he and the officer were facing. It was hand-painted not too long ago, with visible brushstrokes and traces of paint intruding onto the glass of the door's small rectangular windows. Then it hit him with a strange wave of reality, as though he was having an out-of-body experience and suddenly was shot back into his own body; this was *his* front door.

The dark green door suddenly opened cautiously, at first only partially. He heard his father inside acknowledge the officer with a groggy but concerned "*Yes?*" and saw half of a face peeking out from behind the door. He had clearly been awakened from a deep slumber and struggled to gain his bearings so he could figure out who was ringing the doorbell at this hour. The distress showed in the creases of his forehead as he sensed an emergency. "Landon?" his father said incredulously, stunned, now fully opening the door and looking at him as though he'd seen a ghost. He squinted, his eyes refusing to adjust to the bright porch light. "What are you doing?" he asked in almost a whisper, uncertain of why he was keeping his voice down in front of the cop. "What are you doing outside?"

Reynolds cleared his throat. "I found him walking out on Route Six, about three miles east of here."

His father looked stunned with wide, unblinking eyes, unsure what to make of this. He looked at the cop in disbelief, then returned his bewildered stare to his groggy son, who looked as confused as he felt.

Landon heard his mother in the background pushing at his father, asking him what was the matter and then nudging him out of the way to see. Her face dropped when she saw her little boy outside on the porch at two-thirty in the morning standing beside a police officer.

"Mr. Daniels," Reynolds began hesitantly, "does your son have any history of sleepwalking?"

"No. Not that we're aware of." He reached through the doorway to grab his son by the hair on the back of his head and pulled him forward into an embrace. Landon collapsed into his arms.

"Well..." Reynolds held his hands out, at a loss, "I don't know what to say or how to explain this. I would have a talk with him and try to figure out what's going on. It sounds like sleepwalking to me. Get some deadbolts on your doors. Do what you have to. He's lucky I found him. Who knows what would have happened to him if I hadn't spotted him and picked him up. Tractor trailers fly down that road. He was headed in the opposite direction from town, off to nowhere. I asked him, and he says he has no idea what he was doing or why he was out there. Just keep an eye on him. Sleepwalking is a serious issue, and this may be the first sign of it, even if it has never happened before. I would get him in to see a doctor about it, too." Reynolds shrugged and chuckled a little to himself as he turned away to head down the porch steps. "You folks have a great night, now."

Lying in bed in the dark, Landon stared at the silhouette of the bomber plane with six propeller engines that hung from the ceiling with fishing line. His grandfather had put it together for him, since he was too young, and it had flown over his bed for three years now, along with the other models in his room that meant so much to him.

There were model cars, both modern and classic, warships and pirate ships all painted as they were painstakingly assembled so that each piece had its individual color and weathering.

Six months earlier, Landon was staying with his grandfather during winter break when the frail old man passed away in his armchair. Landon was the one who discovered him sitting there, lifeless. He stood staring at him for nearly twenty minutes, expecting him to wake up, to come back to him, before finally running to a neighbor's door. It was a shock that he would never fully recover from, leaving him forever clinging to youth.

Landon found himself alone and confused in the dark in his house with a strange feeling that something was wrong. He searched for his parents though he already knew they were gone. He could feel the evil all around him and knew he needed to escape.

He saw Emily's figure outlined in the dark and a flash of her pretty face. She was still dressed in the genie costume she wore the day before at school.

He called out to her, but she seemed so far away. Though he struggled to focus on her, no matter how he moved or squinted, her image evaded him in the dark.

"Don't let them in," she warned him.

"Don't let who in?" he yelled back desperately, walking toward her.

"Them!" she shouted to him. He could see her figure raise an arm and point a finger at something behind him.

He swiveled around to see a shadow outside the shades of the kitchen window, closing in on the back door.

"Lock it!" she yelled to him.

He ran and slammed into the doorframe, then frantically locked the door and fumbled with the deadbolt.

He froze in place a moment, petrified, leaning against the back door, holding his breath and listening. There were noises coming from outside the door that were like voices, more than one. It was a whispering, a chattering that was just out of his range of comprehension, but as he listened more, he realized this wasn't English, just garbled sound.

The doorknob jiggled. Landon gasped. It moved again, trying to turn but stopped by the lock, one way then the other—then more firmly, angrily. Then the door thudded. Finally, some unseen force began slamming against it crazily, shaking the walls and knocking down the key holder that hung on the wall. When the keys jangled noisily to the floor, the knocking stopped. Landon held his breath, counting the seconds. Then it suddenly resumed more fiercely than before, desperate to enter the home.

"Don't let them in. Don't let them in!" Emily hollered to him in a panic. He saw her running from the kitchen, and he bolted after her, turning his back on the kitchen door that thudded and pounded with such frightening vigor he was afraid it would be torn from its hinges. He tried to follow her, but her image kept fading into the dark, just flashing here and there. Her voice tuned in and out, and he saw a blur of her running down the hallway away from him. He followed her up the stairs to his room and slammed the door shut in the dark.

"Oh no, they're coming," she said as the pounding began furiously at his bedroom door, as though he had no right to keep them out.

There was nowhere to go. They were trapped together in that room on the second floor with nowhere else to run.

"They're going to get you!" she desperately cried to him.

The closet door began rattling and opening. He ran to it, hollering, and threw himself against it. There was no lock on that door. There was no way to keep them out. He screamed as he felt the door being pushed open with each thrust, pushing him across the floor as he screamed out for his mother and father.

Landon shot awake in bed. He realized he had screamed at least twice at the top of his lungs and was sitting straight up.

The light switched on in his room, making him jump and cover his eyes.

"Landon," his mother said with great concern, rushing into the room. "Oh my God, sweetie, are you okay? What's wrong?" She rushed to his side in her nightgown, placing a hand on his forehead, then embraced him so forcefully it nearly crushed him.

"Emily," he said her name as though it was the most important thing in the world.

She moved back from him enough to face him. "Emily? Your friend from school? What about her?"

"I had a dream.... I had a bad dream...."

"Honey, you need to calm down," she soothed him. "It was just a bad dream. Everything's okay now. Mommy's here.

"I need to see her," Landon said, scaring her with the fear in his eyes. His forehead was beaded with sweat, and his hair was plastered to his pale forehead as if he had been swimming. "I need to see her at school tomorrow."

"No, Landon. You're not going to school tomorrow. It would be a good idea for you to take the day off, sweetie. You were out really late, and we want to keep an eye on you."

"I need to go to school tomorrow, Mom," he insisted. "I need to go to see Emily there."

She looked at the fear in his eyes and the longing and gave him a kiss on his forehead, surprised by how clammy it was. "Get a good night's rest, honey. We'll see about school in the morning. Somehow, I doubt you're going to want to go."

2

The next morning, Landon hung his backpack over one shoulder as he walked into the whirlwind of activity in his bustling elementary school. Kids were playing and yelling and bumping into each other as they chaotically moved through the hallways, eventually finding their way to the hooks where backpacks and jackets were hung.

While most of the other kids were in a jovial mood, laughing and yelling, Landon walked through the hall in a daze, anxiously scanning the crowd for Emily. He didn't see her anywhere. She always hung her things on the third hook from the end, on the opposite wall from him, but today her hook was empty.

Landon wandered into class feeling dizzy and sensing something was very wrong. Their teacher, Miss Lundig, announced that it was eight o'clock, and it was time for everyone to take their seats to begin the day. Every schoolboy's crush, Mrs. Lundig wore a dark blue dress today and her hair looked especially pretty as she moved to the front of the room. As the students settled into their desks reluctantly, he repeatedly twisted his body to look back behind him to see her empty desk. He tapped his feet, anxiously waiting for her casually to stroll in late as if nothing was wrong.

Class began, and Miss Lundig told them to open their copies of *The Adventures of Tom Sawyer and Huckleberry Finn* to page seventy-three, where they left off yesterday taking turns reading aloud to the class. He didn't pay attention. He was too busy looking back at her desk every time he heard someone shuffling their feet or moving a book.

Landon turned around quickly in his seat when he heard footsteps entering the classroom, certain it was Emily at last. It turned out to be Damien, his best friend until six months earlier, when they stopped talking completely. Landon noticed his face had marks on it. Landon noticed his left eye was severely bruised, a reddish bruise that usually indicated a recent injury. Several small cuts lined his forehead and his right cheek.

Landon checked Emily's empty desk several more times. He briefly tried to force himself to listen but just couldn't. After they had finished their reading time, they split into the groups they had formed the day before to work on making paper whales. Each group had been assigned a different type of whale to construct out of large sheets of paper cut to shape, then paint and stuff with shredded paper. His group would be creating a right whale, and they were at the point of stapling the two paper cutouts of its body together. The black paint that saturated the paper whale's body sent a strange chill through him, casting images of the blackness of Halloween night. There was frightening loneliness in the swirled, liquid darkness where there should have been a memory.

Landon took comfort in Damien's company now, feeling suddenly very alone in Emily's absence. Landon was glad to see Damien was even moving close to him. He was the first friend he ever had from school. He still remembered the first time he was going to play at Damien's house after school, when he was supposed to take the bus home with him but became so nervous that he got on his own bus and rode home. Damien's mother called over to check to see if he was okay and if he made it home. After that, there were many bus rides home with Damien and many adventures sledding, playing with firecrackers in his yard, journeying alongside streams through the woods, building forts and sleepovers. They had quickly become joined at the hip and were constantly inviting each other over. They thought the same things, loved the same games and movies and often joked that they were almost the same person, causing their mothers to roll their eyes. Then Emily came into the picture.

"What happened to you?" Landon asked him, breaking the ice.

"Oh," Damien responded, surprised, as if it took him a moment to figure out what Landon was talking about. "My face...I fell skateboarding. I was trying out a huge ramp I built with scrap plywood. I landed it twice, but the third time I was trying to do a three-sixty, and I didn't land it right." His tone had almost returned to the usual excitement and enthusiasm in which he spoke to his friend. "I wiped out and slid down the sidewalk on my face. It was freaking awesome." He forced the smile from his face and replaced it with a scowl, reminding himself of how Landon had betrayed him.

"Oh." Landon nodded and didn't know what else to say. His once best friend didn't seem interested in talking to him, yet continued to linger for a moment, as if he felt obligated but didn't know how to get out of it. "That's cool," Landon commented, far too late. "Have you seen Emily?" Landon asked, realizing instantly that it was the worst thing he could possibly have said at that moment, when his friend was actually talking to him again, but he couldn't help it. He knew that Damien was the only other person he knew close to Emily, or at least he had once been. His concern for Emily overwhelmed his concern for his relationship with Damien.

"No," Damien answered coldly, clearly offended. He huffed and rolled his eyes as he snatched up the black paint he had brought over and moved to the opposite side of their right whale, refusing to make eye contact with Landon again.

Landon had met Emily at Damien's eleventh birthday party. As one of the activities, Damien's mother had created a spider web of yarn in between small tree branches. While Emily was navigating the web to retrieve the candy placed as bait deep within it, one of her earrings snagged in the yarn, and she became stuck. Landon was able to crawl to her before Damien realized what was happening. He touched her ear and was able carefully to free her earring of the yarn that snared her. From then on, as Emily was included in Landon and Damien's adventures, Landon had always mentioned how much he liked her. He kept asking Damien if he thought she was pretty, which of course, he did, but he knew he was really asking more for himself.

He remembered the first time he saw Emily walk into their class, with her purple backpack slung over her shoulder and her hair in a ponytail. Landon was frozen in time watching her as she quietly talked to Miss Lundig, seeming nervous and out of place in her new surroundings. Her dark brown bangs fell daintily over her forehead and jostled slightly as she spoke and surveyed the room. She had the face of a porcelain doll, very light and flawless. Her large, glistening brown eyes settled on Landon for a moment, stunning him, making him wonder what had caught her eye. Before he had any idea who she was, he knew instantly that she was the most beautiful thing he had ever seen—and she was going to be a part of their class. She had transferred in from a private school midyear, although Landon never knew why she had switched so abruptly to the public school system.

When the large circular clock on the wall read ten-thirty-three, the principal appeared in their doorway. He attempted to summon Miss Lundig discreetly to the far corner of the classroom, where together they engaged in a hushed conversation, leaning in and whispering. Landon knew he was telling her something bad. He strained to hear but could only interpret his teacher's body language and facial expressions, which disturbed him greatly.

When the principal left and Miss Lundig returned to the front of the class, she seemed very troubled. She said nothing unusual to any of the kids but she was now very aloof and distracted. Her usual joyous, upbeat demeanor seemed to have been shattered in an instant.

3

From within the dark recesses of his home, Chester Thomson heard their voices distant in the woods—*his* woods. At first, he thought it was birds chirping or animals because it was unusual to hear any humans so far away from civilization. He froze in place listening silently over the sounds of the birds in the forest to make sure it wasn't just his imagination; he often heard things he knew weren't there or shouldn't be there—but after searching and waiting he'd usually come to the troubling conclusion that it was all in his head.

He warned his dog, Chip, to remain quiet. Chip stared up at him with one button eye dangling on its threads and stuffing poking out of his ripped seams. His once-white fur was tan and mangled from years of neglect by the child who had thrown him out.

Chester heard a small voice somewhere in the woods...then another. At first, it almost sounded like a woman's voice, high in pitch—or maybe an injured deer or a baby bird squawking for food from its mother in the trees. Then he heard it again, a yell, a holler—and then there was another a moment later in response, calling back; two distinct voices in the forest.

He stealthily but urgently took long strides into the darkness of the room, cautious not to alert these intruders of his presence because he knew his survival depended upon it.

He slowly elevated himself to the window's hole, where the glass had broken a long time ago. He was careful not to let himself be seen, despite the darkness that surrounded him within. He peered out to see who was approaching, who dared wander so close to his house.

There were footsteps through the leaves and more high-pitched voices. It was the *kids* again, those *kids* from town, stomping through the dried leaves and brush, making an awful racket while lowering their voices in a feeble attempt to be quiet, as if they hadn't already blown their cover. They angrily shushed one another to stop making such noise despite the fact that they could be heard a half-mile away. They stalked his home like commandos about to take it over, positioning themselves behind a large tree trunk. He could see only flashes of them, but he recognized them; much to his dismay, he knew who they were.... They were younger when he last saw them, but he knew who all of the kids were.

He slid down further in the window's opening and stepped back into the darkness to conceal himself, afraid that some of the afternoon's light would reflect off his face and reveal him.

As they egged each other on to move forward, Chester was petrified that today would be the day they would enter his home. None of the other kids ever had. They wouldn't get any closer than fifty feet of it, but he knew it was only a matter of time before they found the gall to invade his home and find him.

One child came forward boldly from the trees as the other two watched, peeking out from the shelter of a thick tree trunk. They anxiously watched as their friend moved closer.

Chester moved farther back into the structure, hiding like a frightened animal cornered by a predator.

"Do it," he heard one of the children's voices say from behind the tree trunk, thirty feet back from the boy out front, who twitched and looked like he had no idea what he had gotten himself into. He had ventured deep into the forest to come face-to-face with a monster—and was about to beckon it.

"Come on," the voice in the background insisted, putting pressure on the young boy who looked ready to turn and run.

The boy out front took a visibly deep breath, closed his eyes and shouted, putting his entire tiny body into his words to make it as loud as possible, "Ches-ter, Ches-ter, the child mol-es-ter!"

Chester withdrew like a frightened animal. He couldn't let them know of his presence; although they already seemed pretty certain of it.

"Do it again," the boy hiding behind the tree shouted. "One more time. That was the dare loser," he taunted him.

The boy out front inhaled again and shouted louder this time, "Ches-ter, Ches-ter, the child mol-es-ter!"

There was silence for a moment as everyone waited for a response, including Chester.

There was a sudden snapping of tree branches, a ruffling of leaves. Chester flinched. The boy out front jumped a foot off the ground, turned and ran. The other boys were already fleeing, ready to leave him behind to whatever fate awaited him.

Chester realized it was just a squirrel up in the tree branches, perhaps startled by the yelling.

They all noisily crashed through the woods, yelling to each other, running for their lives all the way back to town.

4

After school, Landon was making the usual mile walk home when he had a very unnerving sensation of being followed. He felt as though he was being watched from every window on the street, a feeling he had never experienced in his hometown. Victory Falls had always been warm to him, familiar, and he had never given his safety a second thought. He suddenly felt very alone on this street, as though walking through a dark alley, and he didn't know why.

He swore he heard footsteps behind him; several times, he stopped and swiveled sharply to try to catch his pursuer creeping up behind him. Much to his dismay, each time there was no one behind him—or anywhere else around him. He didn't understand what was happening to him, but he felt ready to either explode or break down and cry. He began running. There was an evil he sensed lurking, something so foreign and wrong to him that it sent him into a panic attack. He felt there was something he had seen, something he had experienced that was making him feel this way, but he couldn't figure out what that something was. It was eating at his core deep down inside him, souring his insides and making him want to cry. He wanted to be home, safe, where nothing could ever harm him, and he never wanted to leave his home again.

He ran up the steps to his front porch and crossed the porch in two strides. He pushed through the front door in one smooth, fluid motion as he had done a thousand times before. He ran into the entry and stopped abruptly when he saw his mother and father sitting in the living room, silent and still. His mother's face was puffy, and her eyeliner had run down onto her cheeks, although she had obviously tried to wipe it off. There was redness in her face, and her eyes glistened. His father's head hung low, looking defeated, as though he had just been laid off from his job without warning and had no idea how he would support his family.

"Landon," his mother greeted him sullenly. As she did so, his father lowered his head into his right hand as though he had to hold himself up to keep from toppling off the chair.

Landon stared into his mother's eyes without answering. He looked to his father for an explanation, but he didn't lift his head. "What's Dad doing home so early?" Landon asked with grave trepidation.

His mom stared at him for a moment in silence before solemnly saying, "Landon, why don't you come sit down with us for a moment."

Landon entered the living room. He knew by the tone in which his mother was speaking to him and the look on her face that something awful had happened. He feared that he was in trouble and became very nervous; his heart thumping in his chest and a lump forming in his throat.

As he entered, he became aware that his parents were not alone in the room. Landon stopped, stunned to see two other men sitting on the couch opposite his parents, one dressed in a suit and the other a tan police uniform. The tall, bulky man in the police uniform was reclined on their sofa, sinking deep into the blue velour cushion; Landon recognized him instantly as the sheriff who had driven him home. The other man was much younger and wore a stylish suit and shiny tie with vibrant colors. He sat forward on the sofa with his hands clasped together. His shoes were so glossy that they reflected the sunlight from the window. The sheriff's shoes, on the other hand, were brown and dull, aged in appearance and weathered.

When Landon's gaze moved from the shoes up to the eyes of the man in the suit, he winced; there was an obvious reaction in his face, a narrowing of the eyebrows and widening of his eyes in surprise as though running into someone in public who he wasn't sure he wanted to see but knew it was too late—he had seen him and had to talk to him.

"You must be Landon," the younger man with the glossy shoes greeted him in a calm, soothing voice. He offered him a warm smile, although everything about the situation was alien and intrusive.

Landon didn't say anything, just waited for whatever these strange men had to say to him and his family.

"I'm Detective Carter VanDusen, and this is Sheriff Ken Reynolds of the local police department, who I believe you've already met," he said as softly and cautiously as he could, seeming to take great care not to frighten Landon.

Landon said nothing but he knew this man looked familiar. He recognized the creases in Carter's forehead and the way his eyebrows slanted inward and raised slightly when he spoke. He knew he had seen his dramatic features and perfect hair before and remembered thinking the first time he saw him that he looked like an actor straight out of the movies or a TV series.

"You recognize me?" Carter asked him.

Reynolds huffed a little and rolled his eyes. His palms were flat on his belly, wiggling his fingers on his gut.

"Yeah," Landon answered with a subtle nod, amazed that this officer could tell that by his reaction alone.

"We've got a celebrity, here," Reynolds said sarcastically.

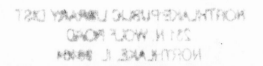

Carter cocked his head and took on an odd smirk. "Where do you recognize me from, Landon?"

"TV," Landon responded. "You were on the news."

"Yes. That's right," Carter said, taken aback.

"You killed the boy on campus who started shooting people," Landon added.

"The *man* who started shooting people, you mean," Carter corrected him sternly but still maintaining his soft tone. "He was a bad man who needed to be stopped." Carter reminded himself to warm his expression and smile. "Landon, the reason Sheriff Reynolds and I are here today is because we need to talk to you about something. We need to ask you a few questions...and now, this isn't anything we want to upset you with and we don't want you to worry...but we need to ask you a few questions about a girl you know, Emily Rose."

Landon's focus suddenly snapped up at Carter, looking him dead in the eyes with fear, confusion, panic, as though the mere mention of her name had surged through him like an electric shock.

"You know her well?" Carter asked as his reaction clearly indicated that her name had triggered something within him. Landon wouldn't have reacted like that if he had been expecting him to mention Emily Rose; he would have prepared himself to appear clueless, confused. Instead, he looked shocked, intrigued, concerned.

"Yes.... I know her," Landon answered hesitantly.

"How long have you known her for?"

Landon had to think about it a minute. "For about a year," he answered nervously, despite having nothing to hide. "Why?"

"How close of friends are the two of you?" Carter asked.

"We're really good friends.... Why are you asking that? What's wrong? Why are you here?"

"The reason we're here, Landon," he paused a moment and sighed, "is because Emily didn't come home last night."

Landon's heart sank. His eyes shot right up to Carter's, intensely looking for an answer.

Carter continued, solemnly, "She apparently either snuck out of the house or was...taken at some point during the night, since Mr. Rose himself had put her to bed. We don't know exactly when she left the house; they haven't heard anything from her yet. Don't worry; I'm sure she's just fine, but we're all just trying to figure out where exactly she might be."

Landon had only a blank expression to offer them. The only friend he had was missing. He had known it deep down the second he woke up from that nightmare he had that something was wrong, but *how* did he know it? He thought for a moment, losing focus on the officer in front of him. It suddenly hit him—why had he known that something happened to Emily? Why had he been so confident that she was in distress?

"We were especially interested in talking to you about this," Carter continued, "because we got word from the local police department that Sheriff Reynolds, here, gave you a ride home late last night. We were told that he found you...wandering around on some back road in the dark, out in the middle of nowhere.... Is that correct?"

Landon nodded, still trying to put the pieces together in his mind to make sense of the nightmare, Emily missing and the police now questioning him. It was all overwhelming, and he felt dizzy, tired. "He drove me home."

"He said you had no idea what you were doing all the way out there or how you got there." Carter shrugged. "Have you remembered anything since you had that conversation with him? About why you were walking that stretch of road at two in the morning, toward Tannersville?"

Landon shook his head, wishing he had more to offer them, but at the same time apprehensive of why they were asking him these questions.

"Do you remember being with Emily last night at any point?" Carter probed. "Or even just maybe seeing her?"

"Nnn...No," Landon said in choked words, his jaw beginning to tremble. He was uncertain of what he was saying and doubted the words coming out of his mouth; he knew he wasn't lying, but something told him he knew more that he was telling them—more than what he *could* tell them. He fought the tears, and his head lowered, trying to hide the fear and anguish that was overtaking him.

"Okay, all right," Carter soothed him, reaching a hand out as if to place it on his shoulder. He glanced over at Reynolds, who shrugged indifferently. "We're not trying to upset you," he calmly said to Landon. "We're just trying to figure out what happened to your friend. You don't know where she might be?"

Landon shook his head.

Carter bit his lip. He held his hands out as if welcoming any information Landon might offer. "Did the two of you venture into the woods last night, by any chance?"

Landon was petrified. He had no idea why. "We don't go in the woods at night," he answered quickly with wide eyes. "People live in the woods. They come out at night."

Carter looked at him stunned, uncertain of whether he should take this seriously or if this was the equivalent to him claiming there were monsters under his bed. He took a moment for Landon to follow up his statement with some other comment, but he didn't. "Who lives in the woods?"

"Chester," he answered in almost a whisper, "Chester the child molester. He's a psycho."

Carter glanced over at Sheriff Reynolds for his reaction to this, but the sheriff offered nothing but a clueless expression and a shrug.

"Okay," Carter said with a sigh, maintaining his composure. He was trying desperately to unlock what he knew must be a lead, a connection, but doing so as carefully as disarming a bomb, remembering to take great care not to push this possible witness away and scare him into secrecy.

Reynolds chimed in, "Look, son, there are a lot of people very worried about this little girl. We just want to find her." He held his hands out, seeming frustrated more than concerned. "But we're having a tough time doing that without your help. We were told that you were seen with her last night. It was Halloween. We were informed that you had plans to be out with her trick-or-treating. Is that right?"

Landon glared at him with fear in his eyes. He didn't know what to tell him. There was a strange feeling of having lived this moment before and a range of emotions washed over him, making him feel dizzy and confused, as though he had been drugged.

Carter could see his face was pale, and he could see the fear in his eyes.

Reynolds repeated, more forcefully, "We were told that you were *seen* with her last night, out trick-or-treating as you two had planned to be."

Landon's mouth hung open. He couldn't even speak to answer anymore. There was something too familiar about what he was saying, making plans to trick-or-treat, their costumes, her genie costume that had made him see her in a way he had never seen her before. He had realized a beauty in her, a feminine attractiveness, almost a grown-up allure, and for the first time he had seen her as a beautiful woman instead of just a pretty girl he went to school with who happened to be his friend.

"Surely you must remember something, son, about what might have happened to her," Reynolds insisted. "Did you help her sneak out of her house? Did the two of you plan to meet later? We need to know the answers to these questions. Her father is extremely upset. Just think how your parents would feel if you didn't come home one day and they had no idea where you had gone. And imagine if there was somebody who could help your parents learn what might have happened to you and where you could be, but that person was refusing to cooperate...."

Carter stopped him by putting up a hand in front of Reynolds' face, first nonchalantly but then more aggressively, realizing his overzealous line of questioning was pushing Landon further back into his shell. If they ever wanted to learn the truth, it had to be lured out delicately.

Tears formed in Landon's eyes with all the pain, confusion and baffling guilt that was plaguing him. What was it they were after in his mind? What did he know about Emily that these officers were so sure he knew?

"I think that's enough for today," Carter said to Reynolds, who didn't look nearly ready to throw in the towel.

"I'm not done here," Reynolds protested. "We have a major problem here...."

"We're done for the day," Carter repeated more sternly. "Any further questioning will not prove productive and I recommend resuming this another day or perhaps pursuing a different avenue."

Reynolds huffed a little, defeated, but also realized Carter was right. There was no way to force information out of the boy.

5

"He's lying to us," Reynolds said to Carter with his eyes lowered in a most serious expression, making it clear there was absolutely no doubt in his mind, as they drove together back to the police station.

"I believe him," Carter said, gazing out the window in the passenger seat.

"You think he had nothing to do with her disappearance?"

"I believe him that he doesn't remember. That's all I can say."

"He's just scared, like a fox trapped in a fence," Reynolds attempted to simplify the situation. "I think he knows what happened to that little girl. He's either scared because of what he did or because he saw someone else do something, and he's scared of what will happen to him if he tells us. Or, now that he didn't say something right away, he's afraid he'll get in trouble for not telling us sooner. He might feel partially responsible because he was there with her. Maybe he helped her sneak out of her house; maybe he talked her into it in the first place."

"Then, why couldn't he just tell us that?" Carter questioned him skeptically. "What was he doing wandering around in the middle of nowhere?"

"He got lost," Reynolds dismissed Carter's questions. "He was distraught. He got turned around in the dark and couldn't find his way back. He remembered what his name was right away and told me the first time I asked him for it. He remembered where he lived. He was able to give me his address instantly. You honestly believe that he wouldn't remember some major incident or accident? He wouldn't remember what happened to his friend?"

"This *does* happen," Carter reasoned with him. "It seems unlikely, but it would make sense that the most traumatic event is what he would forget while other mundane details of the night might remain clear in his mind like any other normal memory. It could be dissociative amnesia or traumatic amnesia—this isn't as uncommon as you think. It could be that the events of that night are so traumatic to him that his mind forced him to forget them, to push them out of his conscience to protect himself from psychological damage—mental overload, if you will. It could be from severe head trauma. This is very real and does happen."

"Conveniently so," Reynolds said with a chuckle. "I think you're right in one respect, that people claim this happens quite often. It's a good way to avoid jail time. So I guess it will just remain a mystery since this kid is refusing to give up any useful information."

"It may come.... He may remember. The memories are there, just not accessible to his conscious mind right now."

Reynolds laughed and shook his head. "You realize how ridiculous this sounds?"

"We don't have options," Carter stated. "Look, if he *does* know, he's not talking. You can't force it out of him; you're just going to freak the kid out. I need him to see a doctor about this. We can try hypnotic therapy to attempt to reconnect him with those lost memories."

"Now, see, when I grew up my father had his own version of 'hypnosis therapy' when we refused to fess up. It was called a bare ass and a belt."

6

"I have a headache," Landon complained to his mother as she tucked him into bed.

"I'll get you something for it," she said as she went to get him some children's pain reliever from the medicine cabinet in their bathroom. As she returned, unscrewing the plastic cap from the bottle, she told him, "I'm going to be driving you to school in the morning. The sheriff and the other gentleman informed me that the town is going to be on high alert until...until they figure some things out."

"What does 'high alert' mean?" Landon asked, sitting himself up in bed.

"It means that minors, children, can't be out walking the streets unless they're accompanied by an adult."

Landon fell quiet. He felt as though the air around him was filled with danger, and it made him wonder what was out there that the police were so afraid of.

His mother gave him two spoonfuls of the syrup and screwed the top back on the clear orange bottle. She set it on his nightstand and reached in to hug him, practically collapsing onto him. She breathed in deeply a few times and sniffled; he expected her to break down sobbing on top of him. She gave him a kiss on the cheek and slid her hand behind his head, slipping her fingers into his overgrown hair.

"Oh my God," she exclaimed suddenly, looking at him in alarm. "Honey, you have a huge bump on the back of your head...." She quickly lifted his head and began feeling it with her fingers, probing through his hair, trying to separate his thick hair to peer underneath it to his skin.

"Oww," he complained at her poking and prodding.

"Did you just get this today?"

"I don't know. It didn't hurt before."

"There's dried blood in here.... You have blood in your hair, Landon.... Is this from last night, when you were out of the house?"

"I don't know.... I don't know," he said hopelessly. He was overwhelmed, and he didn't care where the bump had come from or when he got it. He just wanted everyone to leave him alone.

"We'll get you to the doctor's tomorrow...as soon as we can...." She seemed to stop herself short as if separate trains of thought had collided.

Downstairs, after his mother had finally left him, he could hear the whispering. He couldn't hear what his parents were saying, but they were talking a lot more than usual, and it seemed so dramatic and intense. Every time the conversation began to escalate to the point where he could understand what was being said, one of them would shush the other, and they would both get quiet again.

Landon lay in bed awake, staring at the ceiling, listening to the whispering downstairs as his stomach twisted itself in knots. After a while, he made himself stop listening. He focused instead on remembering Emily, starting with the first thing that came to mind.

He thought about the mansion Emily lived in with her parents. He remembered entering those magnificent doors the first time he was invited to her home, and he recalled how proud his parents were of him. It was as if they suddenly saw him in a different light, as though he had become one of the rich people living in a home like that. Their eyes lit up; their moods lifted, and he noticed a skip in their step for the next few days. They were clearly elated at the thought that they might be invited over some day and be included in such an exclusive world.

Within the mansion's large doors was a dimly lit world of intricate woodwork that looked solid and reeked of wealth and taste. He couldn't believe that this was what they had considered home.

It made him feel sad for his father and mother, who worked so hard to provide for him, but even deeper down within him there was another sentiment, which he suppressed and tried to ignore, that made him resent his parents slightly. He was ashamed for thinking it, but he wished his parents had made it further in life.

Emily's father was the president of the paper mill where both his father and mother worked—although his mother would sometimes say slaved at—near hot equipment with no air conditioning.

It was where his parents first met each other. While his mother was able to leave work for a few months when she gave birth to Landon, she was forced back to the mill due to mounting bills. It was a life of scrimping and sacrifice. They never had much or did much, and it was always an issue of not being able to afford things. They rarely went out to eat, and when they did, it was usually to McDonalds, although, even McDonalds was considered an indulgence that was viewed as a wasteful extravagance. He always felt inferior to the people he knew whose families functioned without giving the expense a second thought. It made him feel bad for his parents and love them more in some ways since they worked so much harder than other people did, yet had so much less. They always just told Landon to stay in school, to get a good job when he grew up, so he didn't end up living the way they did. They had a long way to go, they told him, and there was no way out.

Entering the Rose house was sampling a whole new world for Landon. He instantly fell in love with the lush world of privilege and luxury they indulged in. Mr. Rose seemed to add another rare car to his collection regularly, although kids were never allowed in the extensive garage. Landon had overheard Mrs. Rose complaining to Mr. Rose about a necklace that broke while she was wearing it. Landon thought she was joking when she said it was worth one-hundred twenty thousand dollars. When he told his parents, they seemed belittled and impressed at the same time and told him it was more than their house was worth.

The Rose's were only concerned with making the most of their time and how much enjoyment could be achieved. They had two other houses used as summer homes for getaways and vacations, one in Maine and one in Florida. He had never been to those homes, but he could imagine they were just as lavish as the one in Victory Falls.

Everything was clean and orderly inside. It seemed more like a very expensive hotel or lodge than a home, some place where there was a crew of people maintaining it and cleaning it to keep it perfect for its guests. They even had a butler to answer the door, clean and cook for them. His name was Winston, a middle-aged Jamaican man with large eyes. Landon wondered what it was like spending his life serving someone else's family. He wondered how this man could ever have his own family if he desired, since he devoted his life to the Rose's. Landon didn't feel too badly for him, though since he got to live there and experience it for himself, even if it didn't belong to him.

The Rose family didn't even have to cook their meals. How great, he thought, if his parents didn't have to cook and clean at home. They could play ball with him in the backyard, fly model planes, ride horses at their stable and visit their summer homes when the urge struck.

Everything that occurred in the Rose home was highly structured and regulated. There were no pets in the house to leave hair everywhere or knock things over. Television was considered a waste of life and was not allowed. There was not a single television in the entire home, as far as he knew. Emily did tell him, however, that her father had a rather large television of his own in a closed cabinet in his study, but they were never allowed to enter without him present.

He remembered when Emily had led him up one of the grand staircases with devious excitement. In the stretch of stairs that led from the second story to the third, she stopped abruptly, facing the wall. She reached out and touched a bookshelf with a rounded top. Much to Landon's amazement, it swung open, outward over the stairs like a small door.

Landon peered into the darkness within with more fascination and excitement than he had ever felt before, wondering what she would show him next in this house of marvels.

"Come with me," she said with delight, leading him into the darkness of the wall. She pulled a small flashlight from her pocket and turned it on.

Landon was dazzled by the elaborate system of passageways that ran within the walls of the house, barely wide enough for them to squeeze through. They went up narrow flights of stairs, then descended them. He realized that Emily clearly knew these passageways like the back of her hand, and he wondered if her father had any idea she used them—or showed them to others. He felt like a mouse running through the walls of a house. It was the most amazing and exciting thing he had ever experienced, and it seemed almost magical, like something out of a movie.

"This way," she led him onward in a whisper.

Butterflies swirled in his stomach. He had never felt such youthful excitement and a feeling of being involved. His enthusiasm made him twitch, guessing what other wonders could possibly lay ahead in those secret passageways. He saw a pinpoint of brightness in the wall up ahead, making a narrow beam of light shine into the dust of the passageway.

Emily shushed him, even though he wasn't making a sound. "Look in here." She pushed Landon up to the small hole in the wall.

Inside was as bright as day. It was a room of the house he hadn't seen before, with blue walls and old furniture. It wasn't nearly as lavish as the rest of the house, and almost seemed like they were peering into a completely different home.

Then a figure moved across the room. Landon recognized it as Winston, their butler, only he was wasn't wearing his suit. He wore only black pants and a white shirt tucked in and he was smoking something that Landon hadn't seen before. "What's he doing?" he asked Emily.

"Shh!" Emily pushed him out of the way to look for herself. She recoiled slightly at what she saw in the room. "We need to go. I have to tell my dad."

Together, they stood in his office in silence with Mr. Rose pacing restlessly by the entrance. Then Winston walked into the office.

"Winston," Mr. Rose acknowledged him loudly, irate.

"Yes, sir?" he responded timidly, bewildered. "You wanted to see me?"

"Winston, it has come to my attention that you were smoking in your quarters, and I'm not talking about cigarettes, which would also not be allowed, by any means."

Winston stood like a child in trouble. "Sir? No, sir. I was in my quarters to freshen up and change my shirt."

"That's not what Emily told me," he said firmly, glancing over at his daughter, who stared directly at

Winston. "This isn't the first time she's caught you smoking things in my home."

Winston shook his head. "I don't know how she would know what I do or don't do in my quarters, sir...."

"It doesn't matter how she knows," Mr. Rose snapped at him. "She *does*. Are you calling my daughter and her friend liars?"

"No sir, of course not," Winston quickly conceded.

"This is your final warning. I don't care if it is your private quarters. You're not to be smoking that poison in our home—in the air that we breathe. I don't pay you to pollute our air. I should fire you on the spot."

"Yes, sir," he said softly, lowering his head.

"Thank goodness we have Emily keeping an eye on you."

"Yes, sir," he agreed against his will. He looked past Mr. Rose to Emily and Landon.

Landon would never forget the grave look in Winston's bulging eyes; it disturbed him to this day. He couldn't tell if it was anger, disappointment, guilt...or something else much more frightening.

7

Chester hid in the corners of his house like a frightened animal, infuriated with himself because he, a grown man, and a large one at that, was afraid of some little kids who had set out to taunt him. It wasn't the first time they had come to his house and shouted at him—not those kids, not the same ones, at least not all of them—but *other* kids, who certainly had shared their stories with classmates about the place in the forest in which he was rumored to dwell.

Chip stood rigid, watching his master mumble to himself and occasionally erupt in spastic fits of rage.

That song they created, that awful chant they shouted at his home, had been adopted as an anthem for kids with nothing better to do than look for trouble. They sang that song as if they were chanting "Bloody Mary" in the mirror. It was the song he heard in his nightmares: "Ches-ter, Ches-ter, the child mol-es-ter." It made him furious. It made him resentful and bitter, but most of all, it made him sad.

It was his house, his home, and they had no right to seek him out and invade his privacy. He had taken up residence in the remains of a paper mill that had been abandoned in the 1930s. The mill had been built deep within the Kaaterskill Wild Forest that bordered Victory Falls and Tannersville. The gravel road that once led to the mill had since filled in with trees, rendering the old mill a forgotten piece of the area's history.

Chester had made his home in the middle of the woods to get away from people like those kids, and they *still* found him and harassed him. What bothered him most, what filled his thoughts most days, was how they knew he was living there. Was it just a lucky guess, a story made up by one of the boys with an overactive imagination and it just happened to be true?

Society had shunned him and forced him to live the life of a hermit, and now they sought him out to torture him further, despite having already destroyed his life.

He had done his time. He had spent his year in prison, what would have been a five-year term if he hadn't been released on good behavior. But the prison he found himself in now, living in the woods alone, a prisoner of his own mind and his own anger and resentment, was far worse than his time spent in the state penitentiary. In there, he had some structure to his life, some sense of existence; he felt he was alive, even if it wasn't much of a life. He was around other people, who surprisingly became friends. Close bonds with fellow inmates were forged, but instantly disintegrated once he was released.

The worst part of leaving prison and finally becoming free was that while he was in prison his driving force was the anticipation of finally being returned back to his real life. Now, he had no job, no place to live and everyone he knew had shunned him and turned their backs on him. They had left him behind and forgotten about him. Being free in a world of solitude left little more to look forward to than the eventual end of his existence, which he often fantasized about being sooner than later.

It was through the relative of one of his inmates that he received the help he required, the only reason he could survive as long as he had. His fiancé had initially sworn to stay by his side throughout the trial, believing him, or at least claiming she did, but she later gave in to the pressures of the bad press and her family, who encouraged her to cut her losses and move on with her life. She wasn't the one going to prison, they told her, and she should sever ties with him completely. Before this happened, her parents had loved Chester and were so proud they were going to have a son-in-law like him. He never knew if they really believed the accusations or not, but their perspective on it seemed to be that if he was convicted of the crime then it didn't matter whether he was guilty or not; he was tainted goods and she had better move on with her life and save herself.

She told him the truth was that she wasn't sure she could ever love him again. She knew that all the townspeople and her friends, who were pretending to be supportive and offering sympathy, were really thinking *poor thing, leave him!* She cried horribly for losing the man whom she loved and planned to marry, but felt extremely guilty on top of it for making the decision to leave him. However, as betrayed as Chester had felt, he knew deep down that he couldn't blame her for leaving him. He knew it made sense—she was young, beautiful, intelligent and had a blossoming career. They didn't have kids together. The only thing they had together was their toy poodle, Chip, that he knew he would never see again. Chip would get a new daddy who would take him for walks, give him treats and throw the ball for him. Life could continue for everyone else once he had been removed from their lives like a cancer.

His own family had even given up on him, which was the hardest part. He didn't have much family left, but they had all severed ties with him. They tried to act supportive, but phone calls went unanswered. Letters received no response. As his time in prison went on, he had less and less contact with them, as though they were gradually phasing him out, erasing him from their memories little by little until he ceased to exist, but he still lived on, alone, aside from Chip's quiet companionship, miserable, plagued by his own demons that would never leave him alone, swirling vicious thoughts and hate through his mind day and night, bitter inside and dark as a bottomless pit.

8

Carter stood at the grand front door of the Rose mansion on Main Street waiting for someone to respond to the bell he had rung. The intimidating entrance he faced must have been twelve feet high and ten feet wide, divided into two giant wooden doors with heavy brass knockers on each one. An instant sensation of inferiority had swept over him the second he approached the imperial home, despite his better senses alerting him not to be fooled by such a display of wealth and power. He wouldn't allow such distractions to affect his reasoning abilities and his senses.

The door was answered by a middle-aged Jamaican man in a black suit who swung the door inward and allowed Carter inside.

"Mr. VanDusen," the Jamaican man greeted him. "Mr. Rose is expecting you. This way, please."

As Carter stepped into the dark world within, it took his eyes a moment to adjust to such dim light.

It was dark and gloomy inside, like the Vanderbilt mansion Carter had toured with one of his past girlfriends. It made Carter think that no matter how much money he had, not that he ever would be rich, he would never want to live like this. It was beautiful, sure, but it was also very cold, uncomfortable, and not at all like a home. It was more like a museum or a very exclusive lodge, a place one walked through for a visit, or had a drink, but would never feel completely comfortable in.

His footsteps thundered on the marble floors and echoed off the high ceilings that hovered several stories overhead. In front of them, two sets of stairways on either side of the room ascended to become one on the second floor, and then continued upward to the third.

Carter was led underneath where the two staircases came together through a corridor with fine art on the walls. On the floor were white pillars roughly four feet high that stood to display decorative vases. Carter could not begin to guess how much each of the vases was worth, but pictured himself stumbling over his own feet and falling into one of them, smashing it to pieces on the ground and trying to explain it to Mr. Rose. He watched his step carefully.

Carter was led into a dark room with curtains drawn, deep brown leather couches over an oriental rug and mahogany bookshelves lined with thousands of books with ornate spines. The Jamaican man waved an arm for

Carter to proceed into the room, and then silently disappeared down the hallway.

Mr. Rose sat in his chair staring aimlessly downward, appearing half-conscious, slumped in his seat like a child. He was in his early forties but appeared in his fifties, with his hair quickly turning white. His skin was as dark and leathery as the couches in the office around them.

"Have a seat," Mr. Rose said sullenly, without making eye contact, barely motioning to him to sit in one of the leather armchairs across from him at his desk.

The expensive-looking armchair absorbed Carter's body like a cloud of cotton as he sank down into it. He broke the ice sensitively, "Mr. Rose, I realize what a trying time this must be for you."

"Our Emily," he mumbled, still staring at some unknown point of focus, either at his desk or at the floor, "she was our only child."

"I understand what you are going through, Mr. Rose. I promise you that we are doing everything we can to locate your daughter."

Mr. Rose finally looked up sharply at Carter, making direct eye contact for the first time. "How could you possibly understand what I'm going through?"

Carter corrected himself, pausing a moment and choosing his next words carefully. "I haven't experienced this exact situation for myself. No; you're right there. I've seen families go through this sort of thing many times, though, and I assure you I do empathize with your situation. This is never an easy ordeal to go through. I want to assure you that we are doing everything we can to locate your daughter, Mr. Rose."

"I've looked everywhere." He raised his hands, open, empty. "I've been out searching from the moment I discovered she wasn't in her bed. I haven't slept. She's just gone, gone into thin air. There was no chance to say goodbye—no explanation. I am constantly left wondering what happened to her. She was the sweetest girl I had ever known. She took delight in everything and always appreciated it, no matter how much she was given or how much we had. She was a kind soul and a beautiful person."

"Mr. Rose, forgive me for asking, but why do you keep speaking of her in the past tense, like she's already gone—like you know we're not going to find her?"

"Because if she was alive, if she was just fine, then why wouldn't she come home? Why wouldn't she find her way? She was a very smart girl who could find her way out of the woods. She could find her way to civilization and get help from a stranger, someone she knew she could trust. She was much smarter than normal kids, and she knew how to protect herself and get herself out of bad situations. She was even trained in self-defense and martial arts, but she hasn't come home yet. That's why my heart bleeds because I know if she was just fine, she would be home with me by now."

Carter nodded, unsure of what to say to the wreck of a human being before him.

"It was my fault," Mr. Rose said firmly, more to himself than to Carter, staring off into space again. He seemed a remorseful, devastated, shattered husk of a man.

Carter observed him for a moment, waiting for further explanation, but none came. "How was it your fault?"

He sighed heavily and began deeply, slowly, "It was my fault because I was too strict with her. I was too hard on her and always asked too much. My expectations were too high. I should have just let her be a kid. I should have let her go play and be a child and not held her to higher standards than other parents hold their kids to. Maybe if I hadn't pushed her so much, maybe if I hadn't been so stern, she wouldn't have felt a need to sneak out of the house. She never would have left. She would never have gone out that night, and I would still have her. If I had just let that boy come over more, if I had told her it was okay for her to spend time with him... It was me; it was me being overprotective."

"Which boy was that?"

"That Daniels kid," Mr. Rose answered with aggression in his eyes that knocked Carter back.

"Landon Daniels. I've already visited his home and had an extensive conversation with both him and his parents."

"It was *him*," he said harshly, suddenly unleashing the anger he had been withholding. "I've held back and I haven't said that, but I know it was him. He was with her Halloween night. He was out with her trick-or-treating, and he was the only person she was with, other than that Damien *punk*. Damien..." Mr. Rose fished for his name, "Damien Harper."

Carter quickly jotted down Damien's name.

"It's the only thing that makes sense. He disappeared the same time my Emily did. They probably ran off together, and something happened in those woods, out in the middle of nowhere." He stared with daggers into Carter's eyes, making it very clear what he would like to do to Landon. "God knows what he did to her."

Carter did his best to maintain a neutral, calm demeanor and explained, "We've spoken extensively to Landon and his family. So far, it hasn't provided us with anything that would help locate your daughter."

"He was *with her* that night," he said forcefully, the anger turning his face red. "He was *actually there*, there with her, and he must know what happened to my little girl."

"We don't know that for certain. He was found out wandering the same night she disappeared. He doesn't seem to have a clue what happened to him and he has absolutely no recollection of ever seeing Emily. He doesn't even remember trick-or-treating with Emily or seeing her at all that night."

Mr. Rose stared off at his desk.

"I believe it will come back soon," Carter stated with all the confidence he could muster. "If he was indeed with her that night, I think he will remember. Bit by bit, it will come back. I am doing everything I can to help him, including trying to get him into therapy."

"My daughter is missing, gone, and he just can't remember what happened?" Mr. Rose said as though it was the most ridiculous this he had ever heard. "The only thing keeping us from finding her is that he isn't talking?"

"He *will* talk, Mr. Rose. This is not a situation we can force, unfortunately...."

"I'll force it.... I'll ring his neck.... I'll squeeze his skull until the truth pops out of him...."

"Mr. Rose?"

"There's no respect anymore," Mr. Rose said loudly, slurring his words. "When I was a boy we had...values. We had morals. We respected our elders, and we...we listened."

"Mr. Rose, are you intoxicated?" Carter asked very cautiously of the man in the suit sitting across the mahogany desk from him, trying very hard to avoid offending him or belittling him.

"I had a drink this morning," he answered casually, not offended. "Doesn't a man have a right to consume an alcoholic beverage in his own mansion anymore?"

"Of course.... I understand there was a driving incident yesterday? A traffic stop where you appeared intoxicated as well, significantly over the legal limit?"

Mr. Rose nodded subtly, uncaring. "Is that why they sent you here?" he asked ridiculously. "To discipline me for my traffic stop?"

"Of course not.... I also understand the county let that slide. Carter took a deep breath, held it for a moment and exhaled as if he had taken a deep drag on a cigarette. "Would it be possible to talk to your wife, Mr. Rose?"

He shook his head no with a grimace. "She's not here. She left six months ago, and I have no idea where she went. I think she moved in with her sister, but I actually have nothing to base that on." He belched grotesquely but didn't excuse himself. "Nor do I care."

"Emily's mother left six months ago without her daughter?"

Mr. Rose snorted, and a spastic laugh erupted from him. "That wasn't Emily's mother." He shook his head sullenly. "Emily's mother died in a car accident when she was six. The woman who lived here with us was my second wife, Charlene, who was barely capable of taking care of a goldfish, let alone a child."

"If I may ask, Mr. Rose, why did Charlene suddenly move away?"

Mr. Rose sighed heavily then began speaking slowly, slurring his speech, "Charlene never quite accepted Emily as a part of our life together. She saw us as a jet set power-couple, not a family. Charlene was madly in love with the lifestyle we lived. She was not, however, in love with the reality that came with it. I was quite delusional ever to believe she could grow into a mother figure to Emily. As time went on, it became increasingly clear how little patience she had for children or for anyone else. Our tensions came to a head six months ago when Charlene strongly suggested that we place Emily in boarding school." He shook his head, baffled. "It was as though she considered Emily to be a problem that could be eradicated."

9

Landon suddenly jolted awake for reasons unknown to him. He swore he heard something in the distance, like a scraping of metal. He listened in absolute silence, holding his breath, eyes unblinking, for any further sound. For a moment, he didn't hear anything. Then there was a metal-on-metal click of a lock being opened, and he recognized it as the gate to the backyard being unlatched. He sprang to his feet and ran to his window. He stood on his tiptoes to peer over the windowsill out into the dark as far as he could. His window gave him a limited view of the yard and of half the gate. He could see the gate hung open about a foot. There was no sign of anyone or anything else out there.

He considered that they had accidentally left the gate open. He might have even done that himself or the wind might have opened it if it wasn't latched well. It didn't seem windy, though, but the darkness was deceptive.

He crept across the hardwood planks of his bedroom floor, tiptoeing gingerly to avoid making them creak, pop or squeak as they often did, making a difficult task of sneaking out of the house.

He heard footsteps somewhere. It didn't sound like it was coming from within the house, but he couldn't be sure. He hadn't heard his parents stir in their room, and he didn't think it was them. He silently opened his doorknob, turned it and very carefully pulled it open, unsure at this point why he was being so quiet and questioning whether he should wake his parents and tell them that he thought he heard something and the gate was open. They were stressed and concerned about him enough as it was. He didn't want to wake them up yet again and have them worried about him and questioning him. He didn't want to give them a reason to doubt him if there was nothing happening.

He thought he heard footsteps in the gravel of the walkway that went around the back of the house. He stopped and listened, but then the sounds stopped as well.

He tiptoed to the window at the end of the hallway. He didn't hear any more noises. He ducked low as he neared the window, fearful of whoever or whatever might be in their backyard. He put both sets of fingers on the white windowsill as he slowly pulled his eyes up above it, his eyes now just above its ledge, to look out into the backyard of their home. He gasped for a moment, thinking he saw someone before realizing it was just the birdfeeder and the shadow it cast in the moonlight. It was so dark out that he could barely discern anything in the yard. As he examined the yard more closely, gaining confidence that nothing was out of the ordinary, he began to recognize the swing set, the planters and the two benches they kept in back around the area where they buried Harvey, his pet hamster.

He finally exhaled a long breath of relief that fogged up the windowpane and came out much louder than he expected. After a moment, satisfied that there was nothing there, he headed back toward his room. As he crept past his parents' room, he could hear his father snoring within. It was so dark in his room, though, with the three shades drawn over the window on the side of the house and the two windows on the front of the house. All was quiet and he was convinced he had been hearing things, but the chills still ran through him. He had the feeling something was wrong. It was too dark in his room, and he wanted to let the moonlight in. He went to the shade on the side of the house and yanked it down, then gently glided it upward with his fingertips. Then he went to the window on the front of the house and yanked the shade down. When it went up, he looked out at the moonlight dancing off the front yard.

Landon gasped, shocked. His eyes shot wide open. There was a figure down on the lawn—a large, dark figure standing on their front lawn, right up near the house. The figure's head was tilted slightly back and, although he couldn't see any features, he could tell the figure was looking up at him.

Landon screamed. He cried out as loud as he could for his mother and father and ran toward his bedroom door. He burst out the door and ran into his father, who slumped over and groaned in surprise by the impact, which knocked the wind out of him. The light flicked on in the hallway.

"No! Don't turn that light on!" he screamed at his mother, who looked dazed and disoriented, still trying to wake up and determine what was happening. "He'll see you!"

With a bewildered look, eyes still straining, she asked, "*Who* will see me?"

"There's someone out there! Right out there on the lawn—in front of the house!"

His father moved past him without saying a word, headed swiftly for the front window. He put his hands on the sill on either side of the window and peered out.

"Dad!" Landon screamed in terror, fearing for his father's life.

"Easy, Landon," his father soothed him, turning around and holding a hand out for him to stop. "There's nobody out there," he said plainly, walking to the other window. "There's nobody out this side, either."

"There *was*," Landon argued. "There was a person out there. Just standing there, looking at me...just standing there in the dark...waiting for me."

His father calmed him, "Landon, Landon...it sounds like you were having a bad dream...."

"No—I was awake the whole time."

"Then it sounds like you saw some shadows out there, maybe one of the neighbors' dogs. It could have been a lot of things, but there's nothing to worry about, bud. We need you to get back in bed and get a good night's rest."

Landon pleaded with his eyes to his father but knew it was hopeless. He saw the look his father gave his mother, and he knew he wouldn't believe him or take him seriously. He didn't like the look because they seemed concerned for him, and the concern wasn't because there was someone on the front lawn. They were questioning him. They thought there was something wrong with him. He knew the best thing to do was to get back in bed, which he did.

"Want these shades open or shut?" his father asked in a final tone that told him they had both had enough at this hour and would not indulge him any further.

"Open," Landon answered gravely, knowing they would offer him no further comfort that night.

He pulled the covers up tightly as his parents said a quick goodnight and gratefully headed back to their room for some much-needed rest. They would have said anything just to get back into bed and back to sleep.

He pulled his covers up to his eyelids, peering out over them at the night sky outside. Half-bare branches danced in the moonlight with the cold breeze; occasionally the wind whistled. He watched the window until the sky became light and the sun began rising before his mind finally gave in and fell asleep. He woke up to his mother calling him—what seemed like only ten minutes later—to come down and get ready for school. It sounded like it wasn't the first time she had called him.

10

Carter stood on the covered front porch of 132 Middleton Street, the home of Damien Harper. He waited patiently after ringing the doorbell, pretending not to have noticed the curtains move in the window to the right of the door. Well aware that his presence was known, he was surprised by how long it took for the doorknob to finally turn. He wondered what took her so long to open the door, and if she had considered not opening it at all.

The woman who appeared in the doorway looked much older than he expected Damien's mother to be. He thought that it was perhaps Damien's grandmother, but realized upon closer inspection she was probably only about thirty-eight and had taken horrible care of herself. She wore a faded maroon flannel shirt and ripped jeans. Her dark hair fell carelessly in her eyes, and around the blotchy and ashen skin of her face. Weary eyes were set in darkened eye sockets. "Who called you?" she said very defensively, peeking around the half-opened door as if using it as a shield; her fingers clenching it tightly, ready to slam it shut.

Carter was taken aback by her coldness, especially considering the missing girl was one of her son's friends. It seemed very peculiar to him, her reaction to him or any other police officer, and definitely set his senses on high alert. It is normal to be made nervous by the presence of police, but it is not normal to become instantly defensive and afraid. "Hi, Mrs. Harper. My name is Carter VanDusen. I'm an investigator with the Poughkeepsie Police Department. I'm not sure if you're aware of this, but Emily Rose, a girl from your son's school, has gone missing...."

"Yes. I know. Everybody knows that," she snapped at him impatiently.

"Of course.... It has come to my attention, though, that your son Damien may possibly be of some assistance with locating her."

Mrs. Harper looked at him silently, seeming very uncomfortable with a police officer's presence at her home. "He didn't have anything to do with that," she barked at him.

Carter moved in a little, worried she was about to slam the door in his face. He began to wonder what this woman was hiding. "Nobody is saying he did," Carter explained diplomatically.

"He and Emily were friends. Anything beyond that, I couldn't tell you."

"That's why I want to talk to you. Well, really, Damien. I need to talk to him. I've had a few town residents say that they saw your son with Emily the night she disappeared, two days ago, Halloween Eve. They said they saw your son and Emily and Landon head out together trick-or-treating."

"Yeah...they went out, I guess. He went out with someone; I think it was Emily. More than likely it was her, since Emily is his little girlfriend."

"Oh...really?"

"That's what I always call her. Those two are joined at the hip, or rather, they *were,* I should say. She hasn't been around much lately at all, not like she used to be."

"Any idea why that would be?"

"Not sure. I don't ask. Damien doesn't have many friends at all, practically none except Landon and Emily. I never liked that Emily anyway. She's one of those rich kids in town, lives in that huge white mansion on Broadway. I can't stand people like that, always looking down on other people, normal people like us. I don't care how much they try to play it off like they're not. They're always looking down on us. She's the daughter of Harold Rose," she said with feigned awe, "the wealthiest man in town. We should all be so honored to be in his presence."

"Yes.... I'm familiar with the Rose family."

"But I don't know who Damien actually went out with or what he did on Halloween. I just know he left and said he was heading out to meet Landon. I think Emily was supposed to be there, too."

"Mrs. Harper, you realize that Emily still hasn't been found, correct?"

"Yeah," she said grudgingly. "I'm sure she'll turn up sooner or later. Those rich little brats are always trying to prove something, running away from home. They're the real troublemakers, you know. Not good kids like my son. We less fortunate souls, us poor folk, place much better restrictions on our children. Our kids don't think they run the world. They don't think they can do whatever they want and get away with it."

"You think she ran away from home?" Carter asked.

"I think she ran away from her problems."

"Do you think I could talk to Damien for a few minutes?"

She sighed, annoyed and agitated, as though the last thing she wanted to do was let him inside the house. "Sure. Yeah, I guess." She opened the door reluctantly for him.

"Thank you. This is extremely important. Otherwise, I wouldn't be bothering you."

"Damien," she called him, walking to the stairs. "Damien," she called up the stairs again in an obnoxious tone. "There's a man here who wants to ask you some questions about Emily."

No response came for a moment. Then, a faint voice answered, "All right."

Carter watched a boy appear in view on the stairs, slowly slinking his way down, dropping down each step unwillingly. He had very pale skin and dark, messy hair that looked much in need of a haircut. He wore wrinkled shorts and a stained t-shirt with a picture of a jet flying on it. As he turned at the bottom of the stairs at the landing, Carter could see the bruises on his face, especially around his eyes and nose. His mouth looked as though it had been cut. It looked to Carter like he had been in a bad fight.

Carter introduced himself and told him to sit down so they could talk for a few minutes, to which Damien unenthusiastically cooperated. Damien did his best not to make eye contact, appearing shy and anxious; squirming in his seat like a student called into the principal's office who knew he had done something wrong but he just wanted to be given his punishment and allowed to return to class. He stared at the worn, filthy, brown carpet under his feet.

Carter began, "I'm here to talk to you about your friend, Emily."

Damien's eyes rolled up to Carter at the mention of her name.

Carter wasn't sure if it was guilt in his eyes or fear, or a combination of the two, but his reaction to her name was very similar to Landon's when he had first mentioned Emily. Her name triggered a very strange emotional response from both of the boys and not just because she was missing. There was clearly a lot more to the story.

In this situation, he had to be very tactful about extracting information from children who weren't suspects in the crime and could be possibly upset or worse yet; their parents could prohibit them from being questioned further and the truth from being discovered.

Carter tried to hold his eye contact. "You know she's been missing for a couple days now?"

Damien returned his gaze to the carpet. He turned his dirty sneakers on their sides, looking at the brand logo printed on each shoe. "Yeah. My parents told me. Everyone around town knows."

"What happened to your face?" Carter suddenly changed the subject, trying to catch him off guard.

Damien hesitated a moment and began a word, changing his mind mid-syllable, quickly correcting himself. "Skateboarding," he said softly.

Carter gave a feigned look of being impressed. "That's some pretty major damage. How'd you do it?"

"I was trying to do a three-sixty off a ramp I built. It didn't work."

"Clearly," Carter commented with some amusement in his voice. "Was Landon skateboarding with you?"

"No," he answered quickly with some apparent resentment in his voice.

"No? You two have been close friends for a while, right?"

"Not really. We used to be. I don't hang out with him much anymore."

"Did you see Emily and Landon on Halloween?"

Damien thought about it a minute, clearly buying time and treading carefully, but then realized that this police officer already knew the answer to his question. "Yeah."

"Did you go out trick-or-treating with them, like you guys had planned?" Carter asked him, revealing that he actually knew they had gone together, creating the illusion that he knew everything that happened that night and was simply holding back to see what he said.

"Sort of," Damien answered with a shrug. "We did a couple small streets. We hit maybe ten houses. That was it."

"Then what happened?"

Damien remained silent for a long moment, seeming to be waiting for further prompting. It was as though he didn't really want to say more about that night and felt he shouldn't, but at the same time needed to confide in someone about it. Carter could tell that his mother wasn't very understanding and would never listen to him.

Carter gave him the prompting he needed, "So you guys trick-or-treated for a little bit...then what? Did something happen?"

"Then I left them."

"You just left them in the middle of trick-or-treating?" Carter held his hands out, perplexed. "When I was a kid I would never have stopped trick-or-treating after just ten houses, especially if it was still early. Something must have happened that made you leave."

"There was...something happened," he blurted out, clearly needing to purge himself.

Carter sighed and repositioned himself, relaxing, knowing he was close to pulling valuable information out of him and needing to make him feel as comfortable as possible. "Damien, you can talk to me. Your mother can't hear us talking in here. It's just me, and my only purpose here is to try to learn what might have happened to Emily and where she might have gone. Anything you say could help me, even if you think it won't. The smallest thing could be what allows me actually to find her and bring her back to her family...and friends, like you." He stared at him in silence until Damien finally made eye contact with him. "What happened that made you leave the two of them?"

Damien began tentatively, "She took him by the hand when we were walking. She held his hand."

Carter's head slowly moved back. He took a deep breath. "And this upset you greatly?"

Damien nodded. He then stated, with some anger in his voice, as though seeking some justice, "Landon's mom called her his 'girlfriend' when I was over there waiting to go out."

"Oh..." Carter nodded a little, processing this new flood of potentially valuable information, quickly analyzing it to determine how it fit in with the story. "Isn't that what *your* mom called Emily?"

"Who told you that?" he snapped.

"*She* did," Carter answered factually. "So, the two of them continued on without you, then?"

"I don't know. I went home after that."

"And Damien, what were you feeling at that point?" he asked softly, patiently, trying to get him to open up more.

Damien kept his eyes on the floor. "I felt sad." His body noticeably drooped. "And angry."

"You were angry that your best friend was holding hands with the girl you liked?"

Damien thought about it a moment. "Yes."

"Your mom called Emily your little girlfriend. So is that how you saw her? As your girlfriend?"

"Well..." He looked embarrassed. "Sort of. I don't know."

"How long have you been friends with Landon?"

"Since third grade."

"So, a few years. Did this issue with Emily cause a problem with your friendship with Landon?"

"Yeah. We used to be much closer friends." Damien looked as if he was paranoid his mother could hear him, and he was embarrassed by what he had said. "We used to be best friends. We hadn't even talked for a while, though, until Halloween when we were all supposed to be going out together."

"So, on Halloween Eve, did you get into any sort of fight with Landon or Emily?"

"No. I just left."

"Do you have any idea where Landon and Emily might have gone after you left them? Did you guys have any special hiding places you liked to go or forts you made in the woods or secret places you met?"

"Sort of," Damien answered with a shrug. "We had places we went in the woods. We were never really allowed to, but we went into the woods sometimes and had adventures. We would follow streams until it got dark and then get in trouble when we didn't get home until after dark. We would go to the overlook on the rocks where you can look out and see the mountains way out. We would go by the train tracks and put coins on the tracks so they would get run over. I have one right here," he said with a burst of enthusiasm as he pulled a flattened, defaced coin from his pocket. "We never went in the woods at night, though—never. Not just because our parents wouldn't let us, but because we didn't want to."

Carter nodded, agreeing. "The woods can be very scary at night and no place for young people."

"People say the woods are haunted. That's the real reason why. We were afraid ever to be out there after dark."

"Haunted? By ghosts?" Carter did his best not to sound like he was ridiculing the boy.

"No," Damien replied as if his suggestion was ridiculous. "People."

"What people?"

"People who disappear from town."

Carter began to ask another question but stopped himself mid-syllable. He found himself speechless, uncertain of where to head with this. Instead, he mulled over the strange things the boy had just said, which surely had very little meaning, if any. "Everything is okay at home with you?" he asked him in a very soft tone.

"Yeah..." Damien appeared troubled as to why Carter would ask him that. "Everything's fine," he said with a blank stare.

"Just asking. So, Damien, do have any idea at all what happened to Emily or what happened to Landon that he can't remember?"

"No. I don't know anything. I just left them and went home. I don't know what they did after that," he said, clearly at the end of his wits, not only at being interrogated, which was very stressful to such a young boy, but of the emotions it was bringing up. He seemed bothered by his feelings toward Emily more than anything. "I just want things back the way they were."

11

It was the third day that Emily was missing, and Landon couldn't eat at school. He hadn't eaten breakfast and had a sick feeling in his stomach, as though he was taking a big test that he hadn't studied for, and time was running out. His palms were sweating, and he felt a rush of adrenaline course through his veins that made him want to jump out of his seat.

He felt like everyone was looking at him. His teacher, Miss Lundig, was strangely quiet toward him and had a very bizarre demeanor around him, which left him wondering what she was thinking. She gave him peculiar looks and stares as though she had learned that he was terminally ill and was trying to avoid bringing up the subject, or as if she learned of a death of a close family member of his and was attempting to carry on as if nothing was wrong.

Miss Lundig split the class into groups to work on a word search and crossword puzzle involving historical terms. Landon was surprised and a little intimidated to hear that Abby would be working with him and Damien in their group. Abigail Winters was a blonde-haired girl who was perpetually irritated and always seeking confrontation. She hated Damien with a passion and Landon tried to avoid her altogether.

As their group began shuffling their desks together, Abby stopped and shot Landon a disgusted look. "I'm not sitting with him," she said with a nasty tone, looking down at Landon as if he was a spider on her chair. "I'm not working on this project with him Miss Lundig."

"Abby," Miss Lundig warned her, annoyed. "You're working with Landon and the people in this group today. I don't want to hear another word about it."

As Abby glared at him from across the desk, Landon had no idea what her issue was and assumed it had to do with her hostility toward Damien. Landon wasn't sure if she was trying to confide in him about her problems with Damien or if she was actually angry at him for some reason. He quickly looked away, daunted by her menacing stare. He dared look back at her a few seconds later to try to figure her out and found that she was still staring at him with pure hatred.

"My dad told me that you killed her," she said sharply to him with daggers in her eyes.

That grabbed Damien's attention. He looked at her, speechless, then at Landon.

"He told me you killed Emily out in the woods," she said maliciously. "He told me to stay away from you and your family. And he told me that you're going to go visit him for a very, very long time where he works—in prison."

"Abigail Winters," Miss Lundig loudly warned her as she ran up to her side and put a firm hand on her shoulder. "Get up and move yourself. Yes, take your supplies and everything. Go to another desk—*now*."

Abby quickly stood and kicked her left leg to shove back her chair, which noisily screeched across the tile floor. She swiped her supplies off the table and walked away.

Landon was stunned that anyone would actually say anything like that to him and horrified that this was what people in town actually thought. He felt as though he had done something wrong. Emily was his best friend, the greatest thing that had ever happened to him, and people actually thought that he killed her.

Out of the corner of his eye, he could see Damien looking at him. He didn't know whether his friend was staring at him because he also thought he killed his best friend or if he felt bad for Landon that anyone would say something like that to him. Maybe Damien was watching the expression on his face because someone had finally said to him what everyone in town was already talking about.

"Don't listen to her," Damien said to him when they were leaving the group and all the other students were up shuffling around, chairs scraping across the tiles.

"What?" Landon replied, pulled out of his daze, looking like he was about to cry.

"Forget what Abby said to you," Damien consoled him. "She doesn't know anything. Her dad's an idiot. Don't listen to her."

Landon realized that Damien had waited until the class dissipated before finally saying something in response to the harsh comments Abby had made. "I would never have done that to her," he said blankly in a fog.

"I know.... I know you didn't," Damien agreed hesitantly, as though he wasn't too sure about it himself but he was giving his friend the benefit of the doubt.

"I just want things to go back to normal," Landon said pleadingly. "I miss her and I need to find her."

On his way to his bus, Landon noticed a rusty old brown station wagon driving around the half-circle in front of the school. The brake lights came on occasionally, and one of them didn't light up. Through the windows, he could see piles of junk in the back. The old beater sagged low to the ground on its knobby tires. *What an ugly car*, he thought as he watched it, inhaling the burnt chemical smell of the faint blue smoke it left behind as it passed.

He watched the station wagon round the circle, hitting its brakes sporadically, wondering which unfortunate student it was waiting to pick up. He hadn't seen it before. While his parents were far from rich and didn't drive nice cars, he still felt bad for whatever kid had to come out and get picked up in that unsightly behemoth.

But what was strange about the vehicle was that it didn't stop, and it didn't pick anyone up. It simply finished the circle slowly, gliding around with its heavy engine chugging away at idle, then continued away from the elementary school with its cylinders pounding loudly as it dragged its unwieldy weight to gain speed.

Landon collapsed into his mother's arms as soon as he saw her. She didn't ask questions or inquire about why he was so upset, just hugged him tightly as he sobbed.

He finally calmed his sobbing and said into his mother's shoulder, "A girl said that I'm the reason Emily is gone. She told me that I killed her."

"What? Why would she say something like that?"

"Because that's what her dad told her," he blurted out, devastated.

"Honey..." She soothed him. "That's not true. You just ignore that girl. I'm going to call your school and talk to the principal about that. Even if people *do* think that, they shouldn't be telling their children that, and she certainly shouldn't be saying something like that to you in school."

"But I didn't do anything wrong...."

"I know.... I know. That's why it's so important that you remember. Do you understand me?" She moved him back a little from herself, her arms outstretched, holding him with both hands on his shoulders firmly, looking right into his eyes and speaking to him directly. "You need to remember, for Emily, for you—for us," she said with a quiver in her voice, ready to cry herself. "No matter what happened that night..." she began with great difficulty, barely getting the words out, "it doesn't matter. Whether it was nothing at all that happened or if something bad happened, we still love you...and we're never going to stop loving you."

"But...but I didn't do anything wrong Mom."

"I know; I know," she reassured and quieted him. "We're here for you."

12

Carter was driving alone when he noticed a sight so strange it instantly made him hit the brakes. It was a man pulling a red wagon out of the woods. The man looked oddly familiar to him; he stuck out like a sore thumb in the whitewashed town of Victory Falls. The way the man nonchalantly dragged the wagon with one hand made it look like he had done it many times before.

"Hello there," Carter casually greeted the man with the wagon, leaning out his window as he pulled up next to him.

The wagon had oversized rubber tires on it with mud caked into the tread in the rubber. It was a child's wagon well worn with age, although not from play; this wagon had become a workhorse at some point and lived a very different life than its creator had intended.

"Oh, yes. Hello, sir," the man said back to him, seeming very nervous.

"Hey...have we met before?" Carter asked.

"Ah, yes, sir. I believe we have. I work for Mr. Rose."

"Mr. Rose," Carter said, remembering who this man was now. "You're his butler. You greeted me at the door when I came to the house."

"Yes, sir. I work at the house with Mr. Rose. My name is Winston."

"What's with the wagon?" Carter asked bluntly.

Winston appeared very offended and bothered that Carter felt he had the right to question him about anything he was doing. "I just put some junk in it. I was hauling some stuff out to the woods."

"You're dumping garbage out in the woods?"

"Yes, something like that," Winston said, getting increasingly aggravated and now turning on the defensive, having had enough of being questioned inappropriately. He turned and attempted to continue on his way.

"I'm a detective," Carter replied out the window of his car.

Winston stopped walking away with the wagon.

"I'm investigating the disappearance of your boss's daughter."

Winston nodded. "Miss Emily. I know. The whole town knows about it."

"So you understand why I'm questioning what exactly you're doing pulling a children's wagon into the woods by yourself."

"Yes. I understand," he shrugged and laughed it off. "I sometimes, well...get rid of things out in the woods, honestly, some things that I have trouble disposing of—like oil."

"Waste oil?"

"Waste oil, chemicals. Yes, sir."

"I'm sure the county would love to know about that," Carter remarked.

"Well, yes. I know I shouldn't be doing it. What can I say? I am just trying to make an honest living."

"An honest living dumping chemicals in the woods?"

Winston shrugged. "Arrest me," he mused.

"I couldn't care less about what you're dumping in the woods, unless it's body parts," Carter said with a forced smile and a chuckle.

Winston laughed along with Carter, very uncomfortably. "No, no. I keep the body parts in my other wagon."

"Sure. Well, you don't mind if I take a look at the wagon, do you?" Carter proposed, carelessly motioning to the red wagon.

"Please...I am in a big hurry, sir," Winston protested.

"Just following protocol," Carter griped in a goofy voice. "I'm just trying to make an honest living, too. I wouldn't be doing my job if I didn't look."

"I guess so.... I don't see what the harm would be."

Carter got out of the car and watched Winston become more uncomfortable before his eyes. Carter could sense the slightest change in mood and emotions through body language and eye contact, and everything about Winston's behavior screamed that he was hiding something. Although Carter had no idea what Winston was hiding, he was savoring every second of taunting this man, drawing the truth out of him, knowing that he could never hide it and this man knew it. They both kept up the charade of ignorance.

Carter approached the old wagon and leaned in, examining its interior, which was surprisingly clean and dry, not what he would expect from a wagon used to haul chemicals and oil out to the middle of the woods to be discarded. Out of the corner of his eye, he noticed Winston fidgeting, shifting his weight back and forth on his old work boots like there was something very important he should be doing. Carter leaned in closer, having spotted something in the very clean bottom of the wagon.

Winston lost his patience and complained, "Listen, sir, please, I have a lot to do this afternoon...."

Carter picked up a few of the little white specks he saw on the bottom of the wagon. He rubbed them in between his fingertips and lifted them up in front of his face for examination. He looked over at Winston, who was now chewing at the inside of his cheeks. "Why is there uncooked rice in your garbage wagon?" Carter asked him calmly.

Winston looked confused. "It must have come out of one of the bags I was hauling. I carry food waste too, whatever I need to get rid of."

"There's a hefty fine for dumping out in those woods, not to mention littering on state land."

"I apologize, sir. It won't happen again," Winston said as graciously as he could, forcing a pleasant smile, clearly just wanting to end the conversation and be on his way.

"Well, sorry to be a bother," Carter said to him.

"No problem." Winston remained still despite his body twitching to run away from Carter.

"You have a great day, now," Carter said as he walked back toward his car.

"You too," said Winston as he hustled away with his old wagon squeaking behind him, bumping over sticks and tree roots.

Carter's focus turned to the woods, looking back in the direction from which Winston had come, knowing nothing that Winston said made any sense at all. He didn't have any valid reason for bringing a wagon into the woods. Carter eyed him as he headed down the road and saw him turn his head a few times to look back over his shoulder, making sure Carter was moving on and would not harass him further.

Carter knew he had stumbled onto some very strange piece of the puzzle. Even if it was unrelated to

Emily's disappearance, it was certainly fascinating in its own unexplainable right.

Watching Winston head back down the road with his Radio Flyer trailing behind him, Carter wondered what had really been in that wagon and why he would carry it into the woods.

"I had an encounter with Mr. Rose's butler that I wanted to ask you about," Carter said on the phone to Sheriff Reynolds while walking into the woods from which Winston had emerged.

"Mr. Rose's butler?" Reynolds' interest was piqued. "Yeah, what about him?"

"He was pulling a wagon out of the woods, a wagon with nothing in it."

There was silence on Reynolds' end.

"Said he was dumping some chemicals or waste back there, along with some garbage."

There was another long pause. "Chemicals or waste?" Reynolds sounded perplexed.

"It's a little odd to me...don't you think? The richest man around can't pay a disposal bill to get rid of his garbage and oil?"

Reynolds grunted. "That is weird," he agreed. "I don't know.... I'm going to have to talk to Mr. Rose about that...."

"I'll talk to him about it," Carter interrupted him. "I'm the one who saw him. I want to have another word with Winston, too. I just wanted to see if you knew anything about that or why he would be hauling that wagon back into those woods."

"Huh...? Yeah, okay," Reynolds conceded without much of a fight. "You talk to them. I don't know what to tell you."

13

Landon rode his bike in wide oval patterns so slowly he wobbled and had to keep turning the handlebars to stay upright, making wide sweeping loops across the street from one sidewalk to the other as he twisted his neck back and forth to keep the Rose mansion in view.

He gawked at the monstrous white house with magnificent pillars stretching three stories high in front of the wide, heavy-looking wooden door that belonged on a castle. It sprawled quite a distance on Main Street from side to side, an undeniable statement of wealth and refinement. It was probably the largest home he had ever seen and certainly the largest he had ever been in. It seemed impossibly expensive and unobtainable, something he and his family could only dream of living in, compared to their tiny little two-story home with just enough space for the three of them.

As impressed as he was by the massive structure that was all for the benefit of three people, it made him angry how hard his father worked and would always be at the bottom. They would never have that kind of money or own a home like that, but at the same time, he was awe-inspired by it and it made him want to be like the man who owned it, although he never truly believed that was possible.

He and Emily had been in the process of adding a mountain to Emily's model train layout, which she had received from her father as a Christmas present. He had built it over twenty years but now rarely had time to work on it and had lost interest. It took up an area roughly twice the size of his bedroom at home and depicted an entire town and its surrounding landscapes. Within the town's streets were tiny figurines painted to every precise detail. The layout was so realistic looking that if you took a photo of it without including any portion of the surrounding room, you would never guess that it wasn't a picture of a real

landscape.

The trains were what got Landon hooked on the house in the first place. He instantly had fallen in love with everything in the house and its grandness, of course, but when he saw that train set and spent almost two hours living in its imaginary picture-perfect world frozen in time, he was lost within its innocence and never wanted to leave. Returning home was like returning to school after a vacation to Disney World, not that he knew what that was like, other than the commercials he saw on TV and what he heard from other kids who had been lucky enough to go.

There was even a round hole cut in the center of the layout so that you could climb underneath the table, which Emily showed him as if she was going to show him the greatest secret in the world, and you could rise up into the middle of the town like a giant bursting out of a mountain. Hidden from view from the sides of the layout, behind the mountain's sides, were sets of dozens of controls to drive the trains, turn on lights around the town and switch rail tracks to divert the train to a different path. Landon felt incredibly privileged to climb into the little circle with her and pop up from the middle. There were even little stepstools under the hole to help them stand higher over the layout.

It was the most amazing thing he had ever seen—and actually been permitted to take part in, and there was no adult supervision, no one to watch over them and tell them that they shouldn't be playing with it, that they were going to break it and they didn't have the money to buy a new one. The most incredible feeling of all, though, which strangely came to him on a hot day in July, was the closeness of Emily within that control station in the table where they were confined together. The opening was really only intended for one person, but surely her father took her in there to drive the trains and had since she was little.

He felt her close to him, and it took his attention off the trains in a most unexpected way, since they were the coolest thing he had ever played with. She smelled like peaches and a summer's breeze. As she turned her head, a few strands of her hair brushed his face, making him forget about the trains for a moment and feel warm feelings within him of closeness, of being included, and of feeling connected to someone, although he felt somewhat embarrassed and afraid of the feelings. His face became quickly flushed, and he froze in place, clearly distracted. He watched her play, sensing a special bond with her. He could tell by her face that she felt it as well but was pretending not to.

"All aboard!" Emily yelled as she flicked a switch, making a green and white locomotive begin lugging its long line of passenger cars away from the station. The passenger cars slithered after the locomotive like a toy snake. Looking over at him with a devious grin, she suggested playfully, "We should make them crash," which made Landon laugh. "You drive that one."

While the idea of crashing two trains together did sound appealing to him, as it would sound to any eleven-year-old boy, he was somewhat daunted by the idea of potentially damaging such a beautiful and clearly very expensive train layout, especially being his first time over to her house. He figured it was her set though, and she was responsible for whatever she did with it. He was simply there to enjoy the ride.

"Here. You do this one," she reached over, grabbed his hand and put it onto the control farthest to his right. "Give it half throttle," she said jovially as she pushed his fingers to turn the knob on. He noticed a red and silver locomotive with "Santa Fe" written on its sides begin moving on the opposite end of the layout with a long line of freight cars trailing behind.

"Dare you to actually do it," she said to him with a devilish grin, switching a track. He could see now that their two trains were eventually going to connect, as they were now on the same track, which scared him slightly but excited him. He smiled nervously, and she smiled back at him. She raised her power level, made her train go faster and shot him a smile. He grinned back, realizing what her game was, and dramatically twisted his throttle all the way to high, sending his diesel locomotive roaring through a tunnel and tearing around the track. She hit full throttle as well with a delighted laugh and hopped up and down a little, giddy with excitement of the impending collision.

"Oh no! Jump off the train! Jump for your lives!" Emily shouted right before the two locomotives smacked into each other with a solid crack as his came around a turn, dumping nearly all his cars off the track and jack-knifing several. Trees were toppled; a few innocent plastic bystanders were crushed. The result was a pile-up of boxcars and coal cars throughout the model scenery comparable to the greatest train derailment disasters in history. "That was awesome!" she shouted with a laugh.

"I guess you won that one," he said with a giggle, noticing all of her cars were still on the track.

"Emily," a strong, deep voice said in an ashamed and disciplinary tone from behind them in the train room.

They both turned around suddenly to see her father standing a few feet into the room with his arms folded, watching the two of them with a very disappointed—and angry—look on his face.

"Why did you do that?" her father asked accusingly.

"Dad...sorry Dad," Emily apologized softly and lowered her head.

Landon suddenly felt very uncomfortable with his closeness to Emily, despite how wonderful and new it had been just a few minutes earlier. He didn't know why he felt so ashamed, but the stare her father gave him, looking back and forth between him and her, made him feel guilty as sin. He tried to distance himself from her, but he had nowhere to go, and he realized that his trying to move away made him somehow look even guiltier—of what, he still wasn't sure.

"Emily," her father repeated in disappointment. "What on Earth would possess you to do something like that, to crash two trains together?" From his tone, it sounded as if she had intentionally crashed two *real* trains together and killed hundreds. "Those were *my* trains, Emily. Yes, they are yours *now*. I realize I gave them to you, but that doesn't give you the right to destroy them.

You have to respect the gift I gave you. I worked very hard on that model railroad for many, many years."

"I'm sorry, Dad," she said sullenly, forcing herself to look him in the face. "We were just having fun. It was wrong."

"What's gotten into you?" her father pressed further, now more angry than shocked. "You would never normally do something like this. Is this what you do when this new friend of yours is around?" He gave Landon a nasty glare. "Was this all his idea, to crash trains together for fun? Was this *your* idea or was it *Landon's* idea?"

"No, Dad," she protested boldly, shaking her head. "It was *my* idea. All mine."

"You won't be playing with the trains anymore today," her father snapped at her. "Come on out of there this instant." He eyed the two of them within the hole, clearly bothered by their close proximity. "In the future, maybe you—and your friend—will have a little more respect for your belongings."

A car horn suddenly blared at Landon, seeming just feet away. He looked up, startled to see the front end of a Volkswagen Beetle just feet from him, so close he couldn't believe he hadn't noticed. He wobbled on his bike and nearly fell over, catching himself with his right foot awkwardly, skipping forward a few steps before maintaining his balance. The driver of the Beetle, a portly man with a bushy mustache, shook his head at Landon with a frustrated scowl, which looked amusingly ridiculous behind the wheel of his cute little green car.

Landon looked back over his shoulder at the driver twice, still in shock, as if he couldn't comprehend where the car had come from, despite being in the middle of the road.

Landon kicked his foot and glided his bike over to the curb in front of the mansion, hopped off and let the bike fall onto its side on the lush grass between the street and the sidewalk. As he walked a few steps toward the house and stood looking at it, he could feel something deep within him fighting to pry its way out of his mind. There was some lost memory, some forgotten event that could help her and help everyone in town find her. Although he had visited her house on many occasions recently, he knew there was a piece of time that was missing.

Landon looked up to the large windows of the second story with the flower planters underneath them. The magnificent structure loomed over him, making him feel incredibly small and insignificant, and he remembered his times inside its walls.

The second window in from the left side of the home was her room, which now remained empty. There was suddenly an eerie feeling creeping over him that made him flinch and step back. He saw someone in her room, a face looking out at him just briefly, moving the curtains slightly to peer out. The figure behind the window glass was difficult to discern with the glare off the glass in the afternoon sunlight. He began to wonder if it was just the reflection in the glass of the trees moving, the branches and leaves swaying in the slight breeze, or if he had actually seen someone there. He stared at the window, perplexed, with the uncomfortable feeling of being watched before he took another step back.

There was a noise from the side of the house, further down the sidewalk, which startled him and made him gasp. The heavy iron gate that led to the side of the house slowly swung open with the shrill whining noise of metal grinding on metal until it was open to the yard. He waited to see who was about to come out onto the sidewalk from the house. No one came out.

He stared at it, petrified, already on edge. He backed a few steps away from the gate and from the house, feeling very uneasy as if he had no business being in front of their home and someone was trying to tell him that.

Landon jumped and gasped as he backed right into a solid object where he knew there should not have been one. He yelped as he felt a hand grab onto his shoulder.

"Relax," a deep, calm voice soothed him in a heavy Jamaican accent.

Landon turned and pulled himself away from the grasp of the man in front of him, flinching, before realizing that it was Winston.

"Don't be afraid. I didn't mean to scare you," Winston said gently to him, soothing and calm, holding his hands out as if he meant no harm.

"I didn't think anyone was here," Landon said to him, shaking. "The gate just opened by itself." He pointed to the iron gate that hung open.

"Oh, yes." Winston nodded and flashed a smile of big white teeth. "It does that sometimes when the wind blows if it isn't latched correctly. So, Mr. Landon, what brings you to the house today?"

"I was...I was going for a bike ride. I was looking at the house."

"Oh," Winston said to him sympathetically. "Looking at the house," he repeated strangely as if he didn't believe him. "You miss your little friend, don't you?"

Landon looked at him a moment and nodded.

"Yes, I know. It is very sad, and I miss her very much as well. We'll find her though. Don't worry. Miss Emily is a strong little girl with a heart of gold. I'm sure she'll be just fine. But what are you doing out here by yourself? You are not supposed to be out here wandering around. The police have said so, for all kids. It's for your own safety. We don't want to see anything happen to you."

"I was...I know," Landon sputtered out. "I should get home now."

"Why don't you come inside for a minute?" Winston kindly offered.

Despite Winston's warm words, something about his tone bothered Landon—he felt as if he wasn't being given a choice. "No.... I need to go. Thanks, though."

"Come on," Winston insisted in a friendly tone. "I'm sure Mr. Rose would like to see you at a time like this."

"I have to be home for dinner," Landon argued unconvincingly.

"Just come inside with me for a minute," Winston pressed, the wide smile fading from his face. "Come into the house with me. I can't let you leave alone."

Something deep down inside Landon told him to run for his life—he was not safe—there was something wrong with this man. "Sorry.... I have to go now," Landon spat out, breaking away from Winston's stare and heading for his bike. "My mom's expecting me," he said as he picked his bike up off the grass. "I have to get home fast. I'm already late."

"Of course, Mr. Landon," Winston said seriously, his friendly tone now vanished.

Landon could feel Winston's eyes on him all the way down the street. He kept looking back over his shoulder nervously. Landon always had a very hard time saying no to an adult, especially when they were insisting, but he didn't like the way Winston asked him inside and he didn't like the way he watched him go down the street, as though he was doing something wrong and Winston had caught him in the act.

Landon could feel his thighs burning as he pumped his bike's pedals down the sidewalk of Main Street, uncertain of what he was running from. He didn't understand why he was suddenly so afraid of Winston; he just knew he needed to get away, and he could feel dangerous tension in the air all around him.

His fingers jiggled in his tight grip on the bike handles as he rumbled over the separations between slabs of concrete. He jerked the handlebars back and caught air on one that jutted out high above the next slab.

Landon became aware of a vehicle approaching from the rear. The engine was quiet and was slowing next to him, just slightly behind him. He pretended not to see it and kept up his pace, trying not to pay attention to it, but the sound of the engine didn't pass. It was idling next to him as he pedaled furiously, getting very close, clearly trying to get his attention. It almost sounded like the old brown station wagon he had seen skulking around the bus port. Too terrified to look back, he prayed that it wasn't the station wagon. He finally turned his head quickly, finding the courage to look and see who was stalking him and was partially relieved to see it was a police car. He knew he was safe with the police present, but at the same time, the police meant he was in trouble. An instant sense of fear overtook him.

"Where you headed, son?" a familiar voice yelled over to him from the police car.

Landon slowed his bike and looked over to see the face of Sheriff Reynolds in the driver's seat, leaning out to talk to him just as he had on Halloween. Landon stopped his bike on the sidewalk and dropped his feet to hold himself up. "I'm heading home," he said to Sheriff Reynolds innocently.

"Don't you know this town's on lockdown for minors?"

Landon started to wonder if the sheriff remembered who he was, even though it was only a few days ago he was at his home. Taken out of context, he wondered if he recognized him with all the people he dealt with on a daily basis. "Yeah.... Sorry. I shouldn't be out," he finally responded.

"It's not safe out here for kids," Reynolds warned. "At least not until we have a better idea of what's going on around here, with the missing little girl and all. How about you take a ride with me?"

"That's okay," Landon said, seeming on edge.

"I insist," Reynolds said in a tone that left little room for discussion, lowering his face a little and giving Landon a look in the eyes that warned not to question him.

"My bike..." Landon looked down at his bike as an excuse to decline the ride, uncertain of what to do with it and not willing to leave it. It was one of his few possessions and his most prized one.

"We'll throw it in the trunk," Reynolds said simply. "It'll fit. We'll *make* it fit." Reynolds put the cruiser into park and stepped out of the vehicle.

Landon dismounted his bike and watched as the sheriff effortlessly picked it up and laid it down in the trunk of his cruiser. He was even able to close the hatch after wiggling the handlebars around.

Landon had an unpleasantly familiar feeling as he sunk into the back seat of the police cruiser and breathed in the smell of leather, peering through the bars between him and the sheriff. "I live over on Maple Terrace."

The sheriff laughed. "You think I don't know where you live? You're all this town has been talking about since Halloween—you and Emily."

"Oh," Landon replied, uncertain of what to say to that. It was the beginning of a very eerie silence within the car.

After they turned a corner onto Lark Street that put them two turns away from Landon's home, the cruiser unexpectedly slowed and pulled over to the curb. The sheriff put it in park.

"This isn't my house," Landon informed him, being cautious not to irritate him.

Reynolds turned himself around in his seat, swung his right arm over the headrest of the passenger seat and twisted his upper body around to look back at Landon, who was caged in the back like a felon. "I want to ask you something," he began in a low, serious tone, "and I want you to tell me the truth. Do you remember anything about that night with Emily? Do you remember anything about Halloween at all?"

"No," Landon answered quickly. "I don't remember anything," he said blankly, intimidated by this sudden interrogation.

"No details?" Reynolds pressed. "Still no idea what happened to you or Emily or Damien?"

Landon shook his head no. "I'm trying to remember. I'm trying as hard as I can."

"Are you lying to me?" Reynolds said accusingly, raising his voice. "Are you lying to *all of us*, Landon?"

"No, sir. I wish I was because it would mean that I knew the truth." He wondered how long they were going to sit there and how many more questions he was going to ask. He was at his mercy, locked up in the back of the county sheriff's car.

"Good," Reynolds replied sternly. "That's real good. And let me tell you something," he began in a sinister tone. "If you *do* start to remember things, anything at all about that night, you best just forget it."

Landon looked at him perplexed, uncertain of what that meant and afraid to ask.

"You understand me?" Reynolds said aggressively. "The police won't be able to help you. *I* won't be able to help you, and Mr. Carter VanDusen won't be able to help you. Whatever things you might remember are *best kept to yourself*. You have everyone believing that you can't remember a thing from that night, and if I were you, I would keep them thinking that forever and let it drop. It's in your best interest. If you start remembering things and telling people, it's going to get you in a lot of trouble, son. It's going to get you taken away from your parents. You'll never see the light of day again." He cracked a slight smile that scared Landon. "Understand?"

After a moment in shock, Landon hesitantly nodded that he understood. He was to keep his mouth shut.

"I'll have you home in a moment safe and sound." Reynolds turned back around in his seat and put the cruiser in drive. He gently pulled away from the curb. "Remember, son," he said in a Smokey the Bear tone, "we're in the middle of a lockdown for a *reason*. It's meant to keep a *barrier* between you and evil."

14

Lying in bed, Landon listened to the monotonous gurgling of air bubbles flowing through the filter of his ten-gallon fish tank on the opposite wall of his room. The two goldfish within it stared out at him with round unblinking eyes, making him very uneasy. He saw them as the figures in his dreams, prying to get in like everyone else, refusing to leave him alone, determined that he knew the truth. But he *didn't* know and he didn't *want* to know.

He remembered Emily looking at them when she had first visited his house. She had examined them up close in the glass, getting her face right next to theirs and making fish faces at them, puckering her lips. All he could think was how cute she looked. He found it strange that such a goofy and ridiculous action, for some reason, would make him more attracted to her. Maybe it was because she made him laugh.

He jumped out of bed, ran over and flicked off the black knob that controlled the light on top of the fish tank lid, then ran back through the dark and leaped into bed. He pulled the covers high up to his chin and peeked over them, looking around the room at the shadows that danced from the planes on his ceiling and the model ships that cast an eerie ghost-ship shadow on the opposite wall. His eyes had adjusted, and he looked at the fish tank again. He could still see them. Even in the dark, they hovered near the front glass, halfway up, looking out at him, and their prying eyes scared him even more in the dark. He didn't understand what was happening to him, but he felt the world as he knew it was coming to an abrupt end.

He could not convince himself that they were mere goldfish; he felt something else had taken over their bodies, some sinister force within them watching him up close, gaining access to his bedroom, waiting for him to fall asleep so they could invade his dreams and haunt him through the night.

He reached over and found a small blanket. He frantically hurled it toward the tank, which it landed on and covered mostly, blocking it from view. He pulled the covers back up over his head and over his eyes this time. It was difficult to breathe with the air thick and hot, and there was a musty smell to the comforter that was much in need of washing, but he didn't care. It made him feel safe.

15

It was the fourth day since Emily Rose had gone missing. Carter stood before the grand entrance of the Rose mansion once again, waiting patiently for someone to answer the bell he had rung.

The door swung open. Much to his surprise, it was a young Latina woman, dressed in a proper maid outfit. "Good afternoon," she greeted him with a French accent.

"Good afternoon," Carter repeated back to her, confused. "Where is Winston?"

"I'm sorry?"

"Winston—the guy who answered the door just the other day when I was here."

"Oh. I'm sorry I don't know. Would you like to see Mr. Rose today?"

Carter looked at her, unsure of what to make of this. It seemed very strange that she didn't even know who Winston was. "Yes...yes. I'm here to see Mr. Rose if I could."

"He wasn't expecting anyone, but let me check with him. Please come in." She led him into the massive foyer. "I'll be right back."

Carter watched her head down the hallway, her heels clopping and echoing through the cathedral-like ceilings. She returned only a moment later.

"Mr. Rose will see you now," she said kindly to him, leading him to the office where he had sat on his previous visit. Upon entering the office, he was acknowledged by Mr. Rose, who was dressed in a perfectly pressed suit, as usual.

"Mr. Rose, I was hoping to have a word with your butler, Winston."

"Winston is no longer working at this house," Mr. Rose replied quickly without emotion.

"What happened?"

"I have no idea." Mr. Rose gave a careless shrug. "He was gone yesterday morning when I woke up. All his things were gone as well."

"I would really like to talk to him. Do you have any idea where he might have gone? It's extremely important that I speak with him."

"I don't know." Mr. Rose spread his hands out. "And I don't care. We had our problems with Winston, to be honest. He served us well during his time here, but we had many...issues with him through the years. It is for the best that he took it upon himself to move on."

"What sort of issues are you referring to?"

"Does it really matter?" Mr. Rose sounded irritated, but then sighed and gave in. "We had problems with him smoking marijuana in the house, not to mention always having it in his possession. Where he got it from, I have no clue, but that sort of poison will never be tolerated in this house."

"Anything else?"

"There were incidents with Emily," Mr. Rose stated regretfully. "There were always tensions, problems between the two of them. He seemed very bitter toward her, very spiteful indeed. She was the one who first caught him smoking that poison in our home. She went on to catch him doing many, many other things wrong that got him in trouble with me, when up until then I thought he was the pinnacle of a servant. I was less than pleased with his behavior here I'm afraid. It's a good thing Emily was here to bring it to my attention though. She was a wonderful girl. She always believed in doing the right thing, even if it meant getting someone else in trouble. Winston deserved to be punished. He needed to know his place. And my Emily..." Sobs began to overtake him at the mere mention of her name. "She was a doll. She was such a good girl...."

"Mr. Rose, I'm sorry. Maybe this wasn't a good time...."

"Just find her, and when you do, I want to make the person who took my little girl from me pay. He's going to know the agony that has become my existence. He's going to pay with his life."

16

"The reason I came to your house today, Mrs. Daniels, is to help us all get some answers," Carter said as he sat himself on their living room sofa on the same cushion as he had his first visit. He faced Landon and his mother, who sat like statues on the two armchairs across the coffee table. "I realize this is a very strange and troubling time for all of you and everyone in town. I feel there *are* answers. You strike me as telling the truth, Landon, and I don't doubt you. I don't know what happened to Emily, obviously, as none of us do. But after talking to a doctor about this issue, I believe I know what happened to you and why you don't remember."

His mother recoiled. The mention of a doctor and pushing this issue further seemed instantly to make her defensive. "He said he doesn't remember what happened to him or to Emily," she stated with conviction.

Carter looked at her for a moment, confounded, realizing the resistance he was facing. "There may be a

way for him to remember, though, is what I'm getting at."
His reasoning was met only with confusion and fear.
"There is a gentleman I have worked with before who may
be of some assistance. Sometimes detectives work with
doctors, certain types of doctors, who can help us solve
cases through talking to witnesses...witnesses who maybe
can't remember important details."

"What type of doctor are you talking about?" she
asked sharply.

"Well, his name is Doctor Ralph Jacobs," Carter
said. "He is very well known in this area. He has an
excellent reputation in psychotherapy...."

"No. Oh no. I'm not taking my son to see a
psychotherapist," she protested as she shook her head
defiantly.

"Don't let the term 'psychotherapy' fool you, Mrs.
Daniels," Carter diffused her. "Don't let it intimidate you or
mislead you. We don't think your son is crazy. We're not
going to lock him up or put him on some medication.
They're simply going to talk to him in a controlled
environment."

"I already told you and *he* already told you," she
said with some anger in her voice, "he doesn't remember.
That's all he's said since the second he got home that
night. *He doesn't know*. He doesn't know what happened
to Emily and neither do we. Please, just leave us alone.
Leave my son alone and let him get on with his life."

Carter focused on Landon, whose eyes shied away. "Landon, don't you want to know the truth? Don't you want to know what happened to your friend?" he begged for Landon's help in persuading his mother to cooperate.

Landon seemed like he wanted to answer but felt the pressure from his mother. He knew he shouldn't say a word.

Carter returned his focus to his mother and continued, undeterred, "Mrs. Daniels, we don't know exactly what we're dealing with here.... I understand your concerns for your son's well-being, but what if Emily was kidnapped? What if something happened to her and she needs our help and is waiting for one of us to come save her? If we only knew, if we only had a clue what might have happened, we would know where to begin. We could find her and figure out what happened...before this happens to some other child." He made direct eye contact with the mother, clearly getting his point across to her that this could happen to her own son if this was a killer or kidnapper, without alarming Landon by actually saying it.

"The answer is still no," his mother said with finality, ending the conversation.

17

Carter sat at the side of the desolate road where he had found Winston pulling the wagon, racking his brain to figure out what he had been hiding—and if it had anything to do with Emily's disappearance. He licked his dry lips and realized he hadn't eaten or drank anything all day. He was starting to get a headache. He took a deep breath and huffed it out in frustration, shaking off the confusion. He put his Crown Vic into drive, checked his mirrors and gently pulled away from the side of the road where he had stopped.

There was a loud bang and a sudden impact. The quiet afternoon air was shattered.

There was an awful explosion that sent a shockwave through Carter's chest with the shrill sound of metal on metal and glass crunching.

It happened so fast that Carter didn't even have a chance to react. He was instantly thrown like a ragdoll against his door and the steering wheel ripped from his hands as he was rocked sideways. Carter could only wince and brace himself for whatever he was going to hit as his car slid for what seemed like hundreds of feet.

Then, he slowed to a stop. He was alive. All went quiet. Carter looked around him and found the car was filled with broken glass, shattered into little pellets as it was engineered to do in an accident. The passenger side of his car was smashed in almost to the center armrest. The ceiling was crinkled downward almost to the height of his head.

Pressed against the side of the car was an object so close that it took him a moment to recognize it. It was the grill of a truck embedded halfway through his vehicle, directly next to his right shoulder. He could reach out and touch it and realized how close he had come to death. His body wouldn't have stood a chance against the hard metal of the grill with at least several tons of weight behind it.

A cloud of fumes instantly filled the air with the smell of antifreeze, oil and burnt rubber. White smoke began rising from under the hood. It hit him—he needed to get out of the car—*now*. He went to lunge from his seat but realized he was stuck. He hadn't remembered doing it, but he had fastened his seatbelt out of habit. Looking at the damage of the vehicle, the belt had saved his life since he would have been thrown from the car with the force of the impact.

He fumbled with the buckle to quickly unlatch it and pushed it over his shoulder so he could escape. He opened his door, which, fortunately, still worked, and fell out of the car onto the ground, catching himself with his hands on the pavement. He didn't feel the hard impact of the asphalt and small rocks in his hands, although he knew they would bleed from it. He launched himself to his feet and ran a few steps away from the vehicle. He was concerned that the danger wasn't over and worried that one of the two vehicles could ignite and cause an explosion.

The front of the truck barely seemed damaged compared to his car. It was dented, but not nearly as much as one would expect, given the speed and intensity of the impact. It looked like the dump truck had tried to eat his Crown Vic but realized it had bitten off more than it could chew. Some steam rose from its grill. Carter looked up at the cab. There was no movement from within it, and given the glare of the afternoon sun, he couldn't see anything inside from where he stood. He realized that the door on the dump truck hadn't opened. The driver hadn't gotten out yet, and no one had thought to approach his vehicle and check his condition.

Carter held his abdomen and limped around to the driver's side of the truck, which appeared very old and rusty. It was a large dump truck with a big brown cab high up. Carter grabbed onto the rusted handrail and pulled himself up the steps to the cab. He opened the latch of the driver's door and tugged it open. Inside was a dark, musty cab with a ripped brown vinyl seat with old yellow cushioning peaking through the tears. The shifter was in gear. The engine was stalled out. The keys still dangled in the ignition.

The cab was empty.

Carter backed down the steps. He scanned the area, even the surrounding high grass that lined the road before the tree line. He didn't see a body anywhere. He didn't see any signs of life, either.

He looked back at the cab. There was no way the driver was thrown from the truck. The door was still closed, and all the windows were intact. He looked underneath the truck, and then walked to the other side of it, still keeping a safe distance from both vehicles, with the flammable fumes in the air keeping him on edge.

"There's no plates on the truck," Reynolds said as if saying the sky was blue. He stood next to Carter, who was still trying to wrap his mind around what just happened, with his hands on his hips and his boots planted far apart. "I'll try tracing the VIN, but something tells me that isn't going to tell us much. You have to look out for those 'wild' trucks. They just run right out in front of cars around here."

"So where's the driver?" Carter asked, ignoring Reynolds' nonchalance.

"Probably ran off into the woods," Reynolds answered with a shrug. "We'll do a search, see what turns up. Maybe he just got scared. Some local redneck driving without plates on the truck, probably didn't even have a license, going from farm to farm or something, took off because he knew he'd be heading to jail. It wouldn't be the first time something like this happened." He looked over at Carter and sighed. "Or, I don't know, maybe someone's trying to tell you something."

"Tell me something?" Carter looked him in the eyes, caught off guard.

Reynolds grimaced and looked down to the dirt below his feet for a moment as if trying to avoid belittling Carter to his face. "You're not from around here," he explained strangely, returning his focus to Carter, who seemed oblivious.

"No. I'm not," Carter answered plainly. The tension between the two of them made the hair stand up on his arms.

"There's a chain of command around here, and you...you just don't understand." Reynolds paused for a moment before stating, "I think we have this under control."

"The accident scene?"

"No. The missing person's case of Emily Rose. I think the locals have got this one. You're free to go back to your city and handle your big murder cases and more important matters."

"It's a little girl's life we're talking about. What's more important than that?"

Reynolds laughed off Carter's grave tone. "She'll turn up. We all know she probably just ran away from home. She'll be back."

"I was brought here, sheriff, because this was considered more than a disappearance. There was strong suspicion of a homicide. I don't plan on leaving this town until we either find Emily Rose alive or I find her body."

The corner of Reynolds' mouth curled up. He nodded at Carter with a twinkle in his eye. "Suit yourself, cowboy," he said to him before turning and walking back to his cruiser without another word.

18

Don't let them in, Emily's words echoed through Landon's mind as his heart raced, struggling forward through the darkness that proved as thick and resistant as black sludge and forced him into slow motion.

He had to get downstairs. That's where they were, trying to get in again through the kitchen, through the back door that was all too often left unlocked and provided far too easy access to the house.

He realized he was in the hallway in the dark. He could hear his footsteps on the wood floors creaking. He could see now the dim moonlight shining in slightly from the windows of the front door as he cautiously descended the steps to the slate tiles of the entryway.

They were outside.

He moved through the entryway into the kitchen and ducked down to avoid being detected. He could hear their voices, the strange distorted whispering outside his door. He knew what they wanted.

He hid behind the counter in the kitchen. There were more now than before, and their chattering was growing louder, angrier.

He peeked out from behind the counter to check the door. It was tough to tell in the dim light of the kitchen, but it didn't appear to be locked. He saw one of their shadows move across the window behind the shade, impossible to discern what exactly the figure looked like or what form it had, other than being tall enough to be seen behind the kitchen windows, which were five feet off the back porch. The figure glided across the windowpane, then stopped and seemed to move closer to the window, its shadow becoming darker and better defined. There were three distinct knocks on the glass behind the shade.

He looked around the kitchen for something, anything, he could use to defend himself and his family. He saw the wooden knife holder full of knives on the countertop near the stove with black handles of various sizes protruding from it. He reached up quickly and slid out the largest knife with the thickest handle.

Landon gasped and darted back behind the counter, practically throwing himself onto the linoleum floor.

He heard the door handle jiggle.

He clasped the large knife handle with both hands, squeezing it so hard it trembled in his grasp.

The doorknob shook violently. He heard the latch pop open. The chattering grew louder as they congregated around the door that had been opened. They had found a way in.

Landon stood up from behind the counter and ran toward the door, knowing he had to shut it. He had to lock them out—once they entered, he could never go back. They were coming for him and his family. He ran to slam the door shut and lock it, charging forward with the butcher knife clasped in his small hands. The door suddenly opened faster as he approached—they knew he was coming to stop them.

"Landon!" they shouted at him from behind the opening door with a strange terror in their voices.

He was suddenly grabbed from behind by the shoulders.

"Landon!" the voice yelled at him again, making him scream aloud as he fought whatever force held him. He felt his arms grabbed as well. His arms were pushed down toward the floor as he tried to raise the knife and slash the horrifying force that had taken him.

"Get a hold of yourself!" the voice shouted again, wrenching his forearms with such force that the knife fell from his hands and clanked to the linoleum.

He stopped screaming. He recognized the voice as his mother's and realized she was holding him so tightly the veins were popping out on her hands.

"Mom," he cried to her, turning. Her grip finally relaxed enough for him to move, and he dove into her chest with his arms out.

She held him tightly for a moment, her face pressed against his hair. "This is our secret, okay?" she said into his ear. "We're not going to tell your father about this. We're not going to tell anyone about this, okay? You had a bad dream, sweetie. That's all. You had a nightmare, and you wandered out of bed. You were sleepwalking."

He collapsed into her and wept until the sobs quieted, his breathing became normal and his heart rate slowed. He accepted that it had all been a bad dream, but Emily was still gone. That was a nightmare he couldn't wake up from. She was still with him in his sleep—the nightmare began when he awoke.

"We're not going to talk to those police officers anymore," she said to him. "Do you understand me?"

Landon nodded.

"We're not going to go see a doctor for anything. You told them what you know already, and there is nothing more to say. Understand?"

"Yes, Mom," he said and nodded again reluctantly.

"If you see that cop again around town, that VanDusen guy, you don't talk to him. Don't talk to anyone about Emily anymore."

"They're going to find her though, right?"

She held his head close, his hair under her lips, gazing at the wall behind her, eyes without focus. "Of course they will," she said distantly. "Of course they'll find your friend."

19

It was the fifth day since Emily disappeared. "I really need your help," Landon said to Damien on their way out the school doors, heading down toward the bus port.

"My mom says I'm not supposed to be out of the house alone," Damien said. "She doesn't even want me walking the dog by myself. Everyone says it's dangerous. They say there's someone out there taking little kids. She'd go nuts if she knew I was going into the woods. That's probably where Emily disappeared."

"That's exactly why we need to go there," Landon said.

"There's police out looking for her. Mr. Rose is the richest man in town and probably anywhere around here, for that matter. They'll all be out looking for her. The police department will do anything he says. My mom says he pays all their salaries with what he pays in taxes."

"But they don't know where to look," Landon argued. "They don't know our hiding places, our hangouts or our spots we used to go to."

Damien's head hung low. He got quiet and looked away, suddenly disconnecting from the subject.

Landon sighed. "I'm sorry it made you angry that we started hanging out."

"It didn't make me angry," Damien said defensively, looking up at Landon in surprise.

"Oh," Landon said, realizing he had struck a sore spot with his friend. "All I know is that I need to do anything I can to find her. I think if I go to the places we had gone before, maybe it will make me remember what happened to her. Everyone wants me to remember, but I can't do it by myself. I won't go in those woods by myself right now. It's too dangerous if there is someone out there taking people. That's why I need your help."

Damien looked over at him with trepidation, shaking his head slightly, clearly torn.

"Come on," Landon persuaded him. "It'll be just like it used to."

20

Together, the two boys stomped through the leaves and twigs, hacking their way through the forest using long sticks like machetes. It was just like old times for the two of them, bravely venturing into uncharted territory with an invigorating sense of independence, courage and hope. They pictured themselves epic heroes with shiny weapons and highly decorated armor, charging forth fearlessly through the cursed forest filled with danger and peril.

They hadn't told their parents where they were going. Each of them told his parents that he was at the other's house. Landon knew that they had to look for her. He couldn't sit back knowing she was missing and probably in danger. If she was alive somewhere, wandering around, lost in the many square miles of woods, she only had so long out there alone.

They had set out with their backpacks full of snacks, water bottles, granola bars and an emergency kit from his parents' medicine cabinet with Band-Aids, gauze and hydrogen peroxide to clean out cuts she may have suffered. They knew she was alive, somewhere, and they were going to find her.

Landon knew Damien didn't feel as strongly as he did about setting out into the woods to look for their friend. He could tell Damien felt just as afraid as he did inside, but it became apparent through his body language that Damien was much more willing to let it go and stay inside like everyone was telling them to do.

"I was thinking," Damien said to him as they hopped over a stump. It was the first thing either of them had said in over ten minutes of hiking, "that maybe it's better this way."

"What's better what way?" Landon asked, confused and troubled by this strange statement.

"I mean, that it's just the two of us again. It's like it used to be, and now we're friends again, all because of this."

Landon stopped in his tracks and glared at his friend, who was brought to a halt by his stare. "Why would you say something like that?"

"I didn't mean it in a bad way...but we were always best friends until Emily came around."

"Emily is both of our friends," Landon said forcefully to him. "She's missing. We need to get her back again."

Damien lowered his head, ashamed of having said what he did. "I just want things to be back the way they were before—before Emily came along, before you started hanging out with her...and before I ever met her."

"They didn't have to *change*," Landon argued with him, letting out his frustration.

"After you went off with Emily, when it was obvious you liked her so much better than you liked me, the two of you left me all alone. You were my only friend, and now I'm all by myself. No one cares about me."

"You could have been friends with us," Landon disagreed. "The three of us could have stayed friends. We would never have excluded you from anything."

"Yeah, you did. She did. She liked you more than me. I could tell.... It's okay."

"This isn't about you or me right now. It's about finding Emily."

"I know," Damien conceded, and then paused for an awkward moment. "I just don't think we're going to."

There was an eerie silence with both of them stopped in the trail.

As Landon stared at his friend in dismay, he could see a distant look in his eyes, as though he was hiding something. "Why would you say that?" Landon asked him, shocked and appalled by such negative speculation. It was the way he had said it that bothered him, as though he was simply stating a fact that he already knew.

"Because we would have found her by now," Damien answered plainly with a shrug of his shoulders. "I mean, somebody would have found her by now, or she would have come out of the woods and found someone to help her."

"Not if she can't remember, like me," Landon argued, digging deep to come up with explanations. "Maybe she's wandering around confused somewhere...or maybe she's safe with someone, and she just doesn't remember where she lives or who she is."

"Wouldn't someone call the police if they found a girl who didn't know who she was?" Damien asked.

Landon thought about it, troubled. "I don't know.... Maybe she's hurt somewhere. What if she fell or tripped and broke her leg? Maybe she's in a cave for shelter, staying safe and dry, waiting for someone like us to come find her and rescue her. Maybe she's stuck in a hole.... What if her foot got trapped or something? I think about it every second. I know she needs us. She's scared and alone. I can feel it."

"I...I just...I think this is hopeless," Damien finally let out what was bothering him, "and we're putting ourselves in danger for no reason."

"You can go home right now, if you want," Landon raised his voice at him, his anger surfacing. "You weren't my friend before this, like you said, and you can go back to being alone. You don't have to help look for her anymore."

"I'm afraid," Damien blurted out, realizing he had pushed too far and had offended his friend—his only friend, who he was desperately clinging to. "That's the truth. I'm scared of what happened to her. I don't think she fell in a hole. I don't think she's waiting for us somewhere. I think she's gone, gone forever. I'm afraid it's going to happen to me—and you—if we keep looking for her—we're both going to disappear and our families and school won't ever know what happened to us, just like Emily and then we'll just be forgotten."

"Nothing's going to happen to you," Landon calmed him. "If we just stay together and look out for each other we can protect each other, like we always did—strength in numbers." Landon took a deep breath and sighed. "I'm scared, too. I'm scared out of my mind. I don't know what happened to Emily or what's out there in these woods, but I know what I have to do. I know that Emily would never just leave me out here and stay at home if I was lost."

Over an hour passed of silent walking until they came to the clearing with large rocks protruding that overlooked the valley. They called it the lookout point, and it was where they often sat together and ate snacks and talked about anything but school. It was a clearing in the trees with some open rock face, ideal for picnics or just admiring the view.

There was a faint twinkle in the afternoon sunlight that caught Landon's eyes on the rocks. He moved in quickly to see what it was. It was a dainty gold bracelet with little diamond hearts spaced around the chain. He reached down and picked it up, then lifted it up toward his face. As the gold and the little gems glistened in the sun, he knew it was hers. It was the bracelet Emily's father had given her for her eleventh birthday just three weeks earlier. He thought back to the last memory he had of her. She was wearing the bracelet at that time. The more he thought about it, the more certain he grew. She had lost it within the last four days.

"This is hers," Landon said to his friend in an uncertain tone. He didn't know whether to feel elated that he had found some sign of her, that she had been through here or horrified that he had found it without her, that it somehow had become detached from her. He feared the worst, but he tried not to think about it. She was out there, waiting for them to find her. She was scared and lonely and needed to be saved.

He looked around on the rock face but found nothing else unusual. He searched the surrounding forest and even looked down below, over the little bluff's edge, considering that she may have fallen down and severely injured herself, but there was nothing down there but trees and rock.

"She was here," Landon said more to himself than to his friend. "This is hers.... She can't be far from here."

As the afternoon light dimmed, their moods were rapidly declining, and their hope was quickly dwindling. Neither of them would admit it to the other, but they both just wanted to go to the comfort of their homes.

"We've looked all over," Damien finally exclaimed out of frustration, breaking down emotionally. "There's forest forever. We're not going to find her like this. She could be anywhere. We could keep looking for months and never find her, even if she is out here."

Landon sighed. "That's why we have to look in particular places," he said reluctantly.

"What do you mean?" he asked, clearly having had enough, ready to throw in the towel.

Landon looked him in the eyes. "I mean places she could be hiding, places in the woods that she knew about."

"But we searched them all," Damien said, growing annoyed with Landon's persistence. "We looked everywhere she used to go with me...with us."

"We haven't looked everywhere," Landon said to him in a tone that implied Damien knew exactly what he was talking about.

Fear overtook Damien's face. "I already told you, I'm not going near that place."

"I know she's there," Landon said to him seriously, leaving Damien little choice. "She has to be there. What if he has her there...? What if she's being held prisoner?"

The first glimpse of the old mill could be seen through the colored leaves dangling on tree branches. The rotten timbers of the structure nearly blended into the wooded hillside and trees grew up from within it, nature reclaiming the wood used to construct it so long ago. There were black holes for windows that were terrifyingly dark within. A creek flowed past the mill, down below a small embankment, the steep sides of which led down to rushing water that splashed over rocks.

As he watched Damien fall behind him, the thought of going inside made Landon cringe. The mill stood taunting them, daring them to venture within its decrepit walls and unwelcoming darkness. They both stood looking at it, hesitating, neither one of them willing to take the first step.

"For Emily," Landon finally said, moving toward the structure, having almost an out-of-body experience, plunging forth and ignoring every warning signal his mind was giving him.

Landon ducked down and cautiously entered a hole several feet high where the lower brick foundation had crumbled.

As they pushed their way through cobwebs into the darkness within, Landon was petrified of who or what might have taken up residence within the walls of the old structure.

Although afraid to speak loudly, they yelled her name once inside. It echoed off the old wood beams that let loose dust, which fell like waterfalls as they passed. They moved through cobwebs so thick they could feel the silk strands tearing as they were caught in the traps the spiders set for their prey. Damien spit several times dramatically and swatted his hair and the back of his neck as he passed through it, hurrying, trying not to look like too much of a wimp in front of his friend, who seemed completely unfazed by the cobwebs and darkness.

"I don't think she's in here," Damien said, out of fear and unwillingness to move further within the terrifying structure that could hide anything within its catacombs.

"We haven't even looked yet," Landon said, growing frustrated.

"But don't you think she would come out if she heard us in here? Or yell out to us, or move around or something? It doesn't seem like there's anything alive in here."

Just as he said that, there was a shuffling noise from somewhere within the structure, freezing them both in their tracks. Damien's stick dropped to the floor.

"What was that?" Damien said, ready to bolt.

Landon shook his head. He shushed him without making a sound. They both listened.

"I want to get out of here," Damien said abruptly, taking a step backward.

"What if it was her?" Landon asked him, sounding fairly uncertain of himself. "What if she's in here, hurt or something? I'm going to call her," Landon said, taking a deep breath. "I'm going to call her name and see if she answers." He looked at Damien as if waiting for him to tell him it was a bad idea, to talk him into just leaving. Despite his better judgment and what everything in his body was telling him to do, to leave, to flee, to run for his life, to do anything other than push farther into the dark labyrinth of crumbling brick walls and fallen timbers, he counted to three and yelled her name.

His voice sounded less shaky than he thought it would as it echoed, bouncing around the emptiness of the wood beams and darkness, a sudden burst of human noise in the thick silence. There was a tension in that silence, though that was difficult for them to explain, but they both felt it; they could feel a presence, as if something was very nearby, observing them from the shadows, waiting for them to venture farther inside.

"Emily!" Landon shouted again, louder this time, gaining confidence. He couldn't be afraid anymore.

There was a movement from within the structure. It was a slight sound of wood creaking, like the sound his bedroom floor made when he tried so hard to creep across it soundlessly.

"It came from over there," Landon whispered to Damien as if he knew the layout of the structure. "It was way back there. Come on," Landon said, waving him on with his flashlight beam. The flashlights were not nearly enough to provide them with any sort of comfort, as their tiny beams seemed to be quickly swallowed by the darkness, barely penetrating, giving them just a narrow dim view of the nightmare they were venturing into.

They passed into a much larger room where narrow pillars of light shot down from the ceiling with sunlight catching the swirling dust that rose from within the structure, giving them just enough light to discern the strange shapes around them.

They saw various pieces of things scattered around the room; a hubcap, a bicycle wheel, an old television that couldn't possibly work, and even if it did, there was no place to plug it in. There were mountains of soda cans, beer cans and water bottles piled high in the corner.

There was an old wooden table that looked as if it was meant for children and belonged in a tree house. There were equally old chairs placed around it. There were a few scattered objects on the table: a fork, a bowl, a rag. What really caught Landon's attention were hundreds of books scattered around the table, parts of the floor, and a bookshelf on one wall, overflowing the room as if the person inhabiting this structure didn't know what to do with them. There were a few pots and pans hanging from hooks over the fireplace, which had no fire coming from it, but still gave off heat. Landon backed away, startled. He thought about why it would be radiating heat from its stones and realized that there must have been a fire there recently, very recently. It troubled him greatly and put him on guard. He was beginning to feel very ill at ease in the structure, as they were clearly intruding on someone's home, and that person may not be very far away. He went to say something to Damien, who had forgotten his fear when he became enthralled with the items he was discovering around the dim room.

"Look," Damien said to him softly, mystified. "That's my violin." He headed over to one corner.

Landon looked over at him, having no idea what he was talking about, watching him run a few steps to a corner and examine something with his flashlight as he picked it up.

"This is it," he said with excitement, mystified. "My parents grounded me for losing it. I *knew* I didn't lose it. Somebody took it. They took it when I wasn't looking, and here it is." Damien noticed the stuffed dog standing on the floor near him that seemed to be curiously watching him. Nearly thinking it was real, it startled Damien. Then he moved in for a closer look. It was a filthy stuffed animal that was nearly falling apart but stood on the floor upright like a decaying zombie dog. "Check this out," he summoned Landon. "Look at this ugly dog. This is totally creepy."

"Damien..." Landon called his friend softly, almost in a whisper. "We need to get out of here."

"What?" Damien glanced over at him with the violin dangling from his right hand, confused. "Why?"

"Because somebody's here," Landon answered in a whisper. "Somebody knows we're here. Somebody's watching us."

Landon saw his friend's eyes get wide as he stood up halfway, shocked, and his mouth opened as if he was about to scream but couldn't get it out. For a second, he thought it was because of what he had just told him, but suddenly the wind was knocked out of him. He felt the breath stolen from him as he was pulled backward with incredible force into the darkness by sharp points dug into his forearms and his abdomen. In his ears was a horrifying growling of furious aggression.

Landon wriggled in the arms that held him and pulled him backward, more terrified than he had ever been in his life. He saw the horror on Damien's face as he was pulled away from him into the darkness. He had been overtaken so swiftly that the scream wouldn't even come out as he squirmed to escape the steely grip. He was so slender and agile that he was able to free his arms, thanks to the sweat that had glistened his arms from the long hike through the woods. He was able to wriggle free, much to his own surprise, and ran full-throttle out of the darkness back toward his friend. Right behind him, he heard the growling, the crazed yelling and screaming, the sound of a man crazy enough to kill both of them, drawing them into the darkness as he had done with Emily. At that moment, he knew that this must have been how Emily met her fate, and the horror he now felt was the last thing she knew of this world.

They both panicked and couldn't move themselves fast enough to outrun the howling monster that hurled itself after them through the mill. They bumped into each other and clawed at one another as they scrambled like doomed prey to find a way out. They were trapped.

Landon felt himself grabbed again by a hand that felt like it had claws on it, digging into the delicate skin of his forearm, tearing at his flesh as they both screamed at the top of their lungs.

There was a thud and a crack, and all turned to chaos.

Landon's arm was freed, and he fell to the floor. The clawed hand had let go of him. He rolled and quickly shot back to his feet, fearing for his life.

There was someone else in the dark with them, a tall figure with tremendous power who had knocked down the beast that had attacked them. A black overcoat flowed up around the figure like a cape, like a superhero as he hacked at the beast in front of him. Landon could see now that this beast was a man—a long bearded man who had been blown backward by the punches, landing on the floor of the mill and nearly flipping over.

Landon recognized the man in the overcoat. It was Carter, the cop who had questioned him at his house. The ferocity with which he hit the bearded man was impressive, and Landon was surprised how strong he was because he had appeared rather lanky in stature.

A second later, more men entered the mill and ran up behind Carter. They rushed the bearded man on the floor and dove onto him, pinning him to the floor. The man howled and yelled like a wild animal, gnashing his teeth and trying to claw at them with filthy, overgrown fingernails.

Within seconds, Carter and the other officers had him on his side and were slapping his wrists into handcuffs, although he still writhed on the floor like a snake, smacking into the officers and nearly knocking them off their feet. The man tried to lift his feet and kick one of them, but missed. He was throwing himself any way he could at them, and even when he was handcuffed, the police seemed leery of getting too close.

They finally got him under control with several officers on either side of him and led him out the crumbling entrance of the mill, although he was still throwing himself around and screaming at them to leave his dog alone or he'd kill them.

"You two can't be in here," Carter shouted at Landon and Damien. "Outside—*now*."

Outside, Carter handled the bearded man roughly and shoved him against the ground. Carter bent over to get a closer look at the man, peering into his filthy face. He looked like a bum, dressed in an old army jacket and what looked like leftovers from an army surplus store or something he found in a hunting cabin. His beard was thick and unkempt. The smell that wafted off him was one of someone who has been camping for weeks on end without a shower—a stench of must and sweat and smoke. Carter realized upon closer examination, looking past the mangled beard and dirty face that the man who appeared very old and frail at first was actually much younger than he originally thought. His eyes were young and vibrant. His teeth were perfectly straight and whiter than his own, not what one would expect from a homeless man living in the woods. His features were very symmetrical and sharp in nature—he was not a bad-looking man, and if shaven, showered and groomed, Carter concluded that he would clean up very nicely. He was lean but muscular, and Carter would place him at about thirty-five years old.

"Where's the girl?" Carter yelled at him, getting in his face.

"What girl?" the man yelled back, angry and offended but not scared.

Carter slipped a hand under the left half of his overcoat and pulled out his .45. He cocked the hammer and violently shoved its muzzle into the man's cheek. "Where's the girl?" Carter repeated slowly but more intensely.

"The one who left me and took my dog?" the man asked playfully, but with plenty of resentment in his voice, "or the one who ruined my life to begin with?"

"What's that supposed to mean?" Carter asked aggressively, making it clear that he was not playing games.

"Never mind." The man seemed unconcerned by the gun jabbed in his face, much to Carter's dismay; it almost seemed like he was daring Carter to pull the trigger.

Getting right into his face, Carter asked, "Who are you?" in a stern tone, unwilling to compromise.

"That's none of your business!" the man snapped back at him, struggling hopelessly against the handcuffs. "Take these off me! I didn't do anything wrong!"

"You attacked these boys, here," Carter accused him, motioning over to the boys, who pulled their stare and looked away from the struggle ensuing on the ground, fearful of the man despite the officers at their side.

"I didn't attack them.... They were attacking me," the man argued. "They were in my house.... They were trespassing in my home, and they had no right to be there bothering me. What happened to the Constitution? Don't I have a right to protect my home and my property or have we finally given up on laws?"

"That's nobody's home," Carter said, looking back at the dilapidated structure behind him.

"It's my home," the man claimed. "It's the only home I have, and it's in the middle of nowhere and people still find me out here and harass me and break in."

Carter looked back at the structure again. "You've been living there? For how long?"

"Over a year now," the man stated proudly and factually, as if this gave him rights to it.

"That's just an old structure that needs to be torn down," Carter told him. "These boys here have as much right to be in there as you do, but really, none of you should be in there. That place is ready to collapse."

Carter looked up at the officers surrounding him, who were stunned by the sudden capture of the man and awaiting further direction. "Search that mill," he said shortly to them. "Search every square inch of it."

They immediately sprang to action, heading into the structure, searching for a way in, awkwardly squeezing themselves through the opening the boys had passed through earlier.

"You," he called back to one of the younger officers. "Stay with this scumbag. Just make sure he stays put."

Carter marched over to the two boys and said down to them angrily, "Don't you know what's going on here?"

Landon shied away, feeling as though it was his father yelling at him, but this was far scarier since, unlike his father, this man wasn't in his comfort zone. It was a man he barely knew.

Damien looked afraid, withdrawing, mouth shut and cowering backward from Carter.

"You shouldn't be out here," Carter snapped at the two of them. Do you have any idea how dangerous this is? We have no idea what we're dealing with yet." He took a breath and tried to calm himself. "Do you want to tell me what the two of you are doing out here?"

Landon flinched from Carter's surprising ferocity, which was much in contrast to the calm, gentle man he met in his home. There was an expression of hostility on Carter's face and Landon didn't know if it was from anger at him or fear for him. It made him tremble in the man's presence, though, and left both him and his friend speechless. He had yelled at them the way his father yelled at Landon when he had done something he knew he wasn't supposed to and had put himself in danger with his own actions. "We're looking for our friend," Landon responded in a meek voice, uncertain of what sort of response this would bring from the angry detective.

Carter's chest deflated, releasing his tension through a quiet breath. The intensity faded from his face although he struggled to maintain his hard edge. As much as he tried not to, he looked into Landon's eyes with compassion and sympathy. He saw a young boy who was hurt, confused, trying to do anything he could to help. He saw himself when he was that age. "You shouldn't be out here kid," he said as sternly as he could, but it came out more like a friendly warning than an order. "No one's supposed to be out in these woods. It's dangerous out here, and we don't know what we're going to find."

"Why is it dangerous?" Damien asked somewhat defiantly, calling Carter's authority into question.

"Because I said so, that's why," Carter snapped at him, shifting his focus to Damien. "Look at what just happened. You're both lucky we happened to be around, or we might have had two more missing children. That's just what this town needs right now."

"We were just trying to help," Landon pleaded to Carter, staring at him as though he had the answers.

"I wish I knew what to tell you," Carter said softly to him. "Hey, John," he called over to one of the police officers. "Would you mind making sure these boys make it home safely?"

"No problem," the officer answered him, heading over. "Let's get you guys home," he said to the boys, waving for them to follow him.

"Look, I appreciate your efforts," Carter said to the boys as they were led away, "and I'm sure Emily's family would appreciate what you're doing, but you just leave that up to us. You belong at home behind locked doors, at least until we figure out what's going on around here."

"Don't I have the right to a lawyer?" the bearded man asked obnoxiously.

"You have an attorney you'd like to call?" Carter replied, somewhat amused.

The man was silent, but the sneer remained on his lips.

"Where is she?" Carter asked, his tone getting more serious.

"Who?" the man shouted at him angrily.

"You know who I'm talking about," Carter snapped back. "Emily Rose."

Chester's face went cold. The anger bled from him. His lips relaxed and covered his gnashed teeth. His eyebrows slanted inward slightly.

"Where is Emily?" Carter asked again, knowing by how stunned he was by the mere mention of her name that he had some connection to her. He knew exactly whom Carter was talking about.

"How should I know where she is?" Chester answered with surprising resentment in his voice. "Why are you asking *me that*?"

"You know who she is, right?" Carter insisted, knowing he had him pegged.

"I know who she is all right. How could I forget?" He huffed. "She ruined my life. She took everything from me."

Carter looked at him strangely, giving him a chance to talk. This was not the response he had been expecting at all.

"She's the reason I'm living in the woods," he continued bitterly. "She's the reason I'm living in isolation like a freak. She *made* me into a freak. She's the reason I went to prison for a year, and the hell I faced in prison was nothing compared to the living hell I'm in now. I just want to be left alone."

"What did Emily do to you?" Carter asked without emotion, waiting for answers.

"She put me here. She put me in prison and she put me in this hell I live in now, this social isolation nightmare. She accused me of doing things to her, unspeakable things I would never do to any child, ever. She blackmailed me. It was over nothing.... She ruined my life over *nothing*. She was going to get in trouble because I caught her cheating. I was going to have a meeting and tell her father what she had done. It wasn't the first time I had had a problem with her, but this was the most serious thing I had caught her doing, and she was scared. She was very scared of what her father would think of her and what he would do. So, she threatened me not to get her in trouble. She told me that if I did that, she would tell everyone that I touched her in bad places. She told me that no one would believe me if I said I didn't do it, and she was right about that— they didn't. She told me her father was the most powerful man in the county, which I already knew, and that he would make sure she sent me to prison for the rest of my life when he found out. I was scared, I admit. I was very worried that she would really do it, that what she was saying was true, but at that moment, I refused to back down to a ten-year-old. I told her that there was nothing to talk about, that I had caught her and I would take the appropriate steps to discipline her for what she had done.

I wasn't going to be intimidated and threatened by a student, especially when the threats were of that obscene nature. It seemed horribly wrong to even consider giving in, but now I wish more than anything that I had. It wouldn't have been that big of a deal. I should have just let it go. God, if I had known what this would do to my life, I would have just done the morally incorrect thing and let it go. I could have saved everything. I could have forgotten it and moved on with my life. I would love to say there was some lesson learned by sticking to my guns and doing what was right in the situation, but nothing good came out of it—for anyone."

Carter was silent for a moment, stunned. "I hadn't heard anything about this before."

"It was kept very quiet. Her father made sure of that. He didn't want everyone within a twenty-mile radius thinking his daughter had been molested, even though in his mind she had done nothing wrong. He went to great lengths with the town officials to keep the whole situation under wraps."

"You realize what you're saying is difficult to believe?"

"Look me up in the police records—Chester Thompson," Chester offered. "You don't understand what was wrong with that girl. The side of her I saw...it was evil, vicious. She was a little monster created by her father, who had given her this overinflated sense of self-worth, this illusion of being a goddess, as he considered himself to be a god in this community."

"It seems you would have a strong motivation to make her disappear, then," Carter suggested.

"No. I resent them. I resent her and her father for what they did to me. You might even say I hate them for it, but I would never do anything to hurt anyone, especially not a child. That would put me on their level, and I would never stoop that low."

The police officers emerged from the mill and walked back over to Carter and the boys. "We didn't find anything in there," one of them said to Carter. "No girl, no sign that she has been here at any point, not much of anything."

Carter nodded sullenly, looking back at him. "We don't have anything to hold this guy on. I have motive, but I don't have anything to back that up."

"I know who that was," Damien said to Landon on their way out of the woods once the officer had left them, instantly grabbing Landon's attention. "It was Chester."

"Chester?" Landon stopped walking and faced Damien. "Chester the child molester?"

"I know because Emily told me all about it. I know everything that happened. She swore me to secrecy, though."

It bothered Landon slightly that she had trusted Damien with such an important secret, reminding him how close they had once been. He shoved that thought back in his mind, realizing how trivial such rivalry was at a time like this. "What did Emily have to do with Chester?"

"She was the one who put him in prison," Damien said bluntly. "She said he did things to her. She's the reason he lives in the woods."

"That happened to Emily?" Landon was shocked, angry and devastated that the girl he felt so strongly about had been through such an awful and scarring ordeal.

"It *didn't* happen," Damien corrected him. "She just *said* that it did. Chester never did anything to her. She lied about it to avoid getting in trouble when he was her math teacher. She told me what she did. She felt terrible about it and didn't know what to do, but she couldn't take it back once she had done it."

"Why didn't you tell me this sooner?" Landon said. "Why didn't you do anything to help Chester?"

"She swore me to secrecy. That's what she wanted. I was the only person in the world who she told, just me and her diary—and I'm the only person in the world who knows where that diary is."

"But look what it did to Chester," Landon said as his heart bled for the wreck of a man they encountered in the mill.

"I should have said something." Damien shook his head. "Emily was everything to me back then and I guess it meant so much to me that she knew she could trust me. No one else has ever trusted me with anything. I realized that it was wrong when I saw Chester's face on the news. I didn't say anything later because I was afraid. I blocked it out and pretended I didn't know anything about it. I wasn't supposed to know. I couldn't explain how I knew, and I didn't want to get in trouble." He lowered his head. "I wish Emily had never told me."

21

It was the sixth day that Emily had been missing. The bus line was packed bumper to bumper with cars, all with moms and dads anxiously scanning the doors for their children to emerge from the school and make the short walk from the exits to their car doors.

The buses waited in line, seemingly empty with less than a quarter of the seats filled. There were rows of empty windows with only a few small faces with worried eyes peering out from behind the glass. They were the forgotten children, the ones whose parents either didn't watch the news, couldn't find a way to pick them up from school themselves, refused to give in to threats or simply didn't care.

Clouds of unfiltered bus exhaust mixed with the pungent smell of asphalt baking in the sun. The sound of kids yelling and laughing was barely audible over bus engines roaring as they pulled away.

"We can't give up looking. I'll be out every day if I have to," Landon said to Damien as they were about to part ways toward their separate buses. "I don't care about any lockdown."

Damien lowered his head slightly, clearly troubled by the thought of venturing back into the woods after what happened with Chester—and after Carter warned them not to do it again. "I'll be right there with you," he said bravely, looking his best friend in the eyes before they slapped hands and headed toward their buses.

Landon's bus was first; he hopped up the steps into the familiarly unpleasant smell of a school bus—the pungent odor of vinyl and rubber. He swung into an empty seat and slid over by the window. From where he sat, he could clearly see the red backpack of his friend moving through the crowd toward his bus. He looked at him and felt awful for what he had done to him. He knew he had hurt him badly, and their relationship would never be the same.

Then he saw Damien stop and hesitate, looking over at a vehicle pulled up next to him. He wondered whom he was talking to in the car, who had gotten his attention. He could see only the side of the vehicle and knew what it was, although he didn't know the exact model of the car or the make. He knew he had seen that vehicle before, though he couldn't remember when or where. It was an old vehicle, a tan-brown station wagon with rust along its bottom panels, unwashed, that definitely stuck out from the other cars in town. A lot of people drove beat up cars in town that you normally wouldn't see in other more affluent areas, but it was rare to see anyone drive a car that dilapidated.

Landon remembered the rusty tailpipe hanging off to one side like a cigar hanging loosely out of the corner of its mouth, puffing out wafts of blue exhaust. It was riddled with rot eating at its old body.

The taillights were almost droopy and sad in appearance against the obese body of the wagon. He could see through a large window across the back that the trunk area was packed full of things inside, although he couldn't tell what.

He saw Damien look around, anxiously, almost as if the driver was asking him for directions.

Landon knew that wasn't Damien's mother's car. She drove a burgundy Buick.

He saw Damien look both ways.

Landon tensed up, moving closer to the bus window. His face pushed against the glass. His breath fogged it up and he anxiously wiped it away to see. He began to panic. He should do something. *He had to do something.*

Damien hesitated, stepping a few paces back and forth.

Landon could see it in his face, even from the distance, that he wasn't sure what to do.

Don't do it, Landon screamed in his head.

Damien moved closer to the station wagon.

No, Landon yelled in his mind. He saw him reach out for the door handle.

No, no!

The door pulled open.

Landon jumped in his seat, clutching the green rubber of the seat in front of him, digging his fingernails into it and leaving indents.

The station wagon's door closed.

"Wait!" Landon shouted up to the bus driver, who glanced back at him in her oversized mirror. He ran up the bus isle, snagging and nearly tripping over the shoulder strap of someone's backpack. He grabbed the pole at the front of the isle with his right hand and swung himself down the steps, skipping all the steps and landing on the sidewalk below with a thud, nearly knocking him off his feet, onto the dirty black pavement in need of repaving below. He ran out over the sidewalk into the grass to get a better angle to see, then ran in the direction that he last saw his friend.

He stretched his neck upward to see over the other students passing by, who were all hurrying to make their buses or find the vehicles waiting for them.

The station wagon was gone. In its place sat a red sedan idling. He kept scanning the line anyway, thinking somehow he had missed it, but it wasn't there. He tried to reassure himself that it was a friend of Damien's or a relative, even a neighbor, who had come to pick him up from school that day rather than have him ride the bus. He had a sick feeling in his stomach, though, that warned him that something was very wrong.

Inside the school, no one else had noticed the brown station wagon or had seen Damien enter it. They had no idea what Landon was talking about when he ran into the principal's office hollering sentence fragments, but after seeing how hysterical he was, they quickly interrogated him and phoned the police.

They held Landon's bus for him until the faculty sent him home. They told him not to worry, that it was most likely someone Damien knew giving him a ride home instead of having him take the bus. The school was desperately trying to contact Damien's mother when Landon left the office, but she normally worked days and they were having trouble reaching her.

On the ride home, Landon reassured himself that his friend would never have entered a stranger's car, especially when the town was on high alert for missing children. Damien was far too smart and cautious.

Landon received the news from his mother that evening that Damien never returned home from school. The phone rang endlessly. His mother repeated the same morbid conversation until Landon couldn't listen anymore.

Carter VanDusen was at their front door not ten minutes later. Landon gave him the best description he could of the station wagon. He told him he had seen it once before in the circle in front his school, skulking slowly without picking up anyone. Carter was thirsty for any details he could give him, but there came a point when there was nothing more to give. Landon wasn't able to copy down the license plate. He hadn't seen the driver of the vehicle. He didn't even know the make and model of the wagon.

Landon had been there to witness his friend being snatched away and now he was totally helpless. He should have done something. He would give anything for another chance to do *something* to help his friend instead of watching him disappear.

22

It was the seventh day since Emily disappeared. Landon was walking along the cracked broken sidewalk, focusing on not tripping over the broken pieces as he had done a dozen times before, hoping no police saw him and asked him what he was doing out. He felt the hardness of the closed Swiss Army knife in his pants pocket to verify that it hadn't slipped out. It was giving him a false sense of confidence and made him feel he was safe out walking.

He only had one thought in his mind: *No one else was going to find his friends.*

He was passing the Getty gas station with the outdated gas pumps and the ugly white paint chipping off the structure when he saw something that stood out to him instantly as a sign of danger. It set him on high alert like the sight of a shark fin in water. It was the car he had seen before, there was no doubt in his mind—the ugly old brown station wagon rotting with rust.

It sat idling with its big old monstrosity of an engine chugging away, with the firing of the big cylinders sounding like helicopter blades chopping through the air in the distance. Landon stopped in the middle of the sidewalk. Despite having seen only half of it when Damien got into it at the bus port, he knew it was the same car. He held a hand up in front of his face to cover half his vision and adjusted it until it was blocking half the vehicle. The taillights were the same. The exhaust pipe was corroded, hanging out like a cigar of an old country bumpkin.

This vehicle that had stolen his friends, now sat empty, right in front of him. He thought about calling the police or that investigator, Carter, but he knew there was nothing they could do. They would take too long to arrive anyhow, and had nothing to go on. They certainly could not arrest the driver on the spot because of Landon's very vague description of the right quarter of his vehicle, which he had only seen for a moment, and he hadn't gotten anything other than a description of the taillights and back window.

He could never convince anyone else of it, but he was certain it was the car that had swallowed up his friends. Wherever that car came from, wherever it was heading, it could lead him to them.

The long rear window of the wagon was rolled down, which was a feature of that particular model. He looked at the windows of the convenience store to see if he could spot the driver in there, but the glare of the afternoon sunlight against the glass of the store made it difficult to see inside. He could see several silhouettes of people inside and someone standing in line at the counter, perhaps talking or ordering coffee or cigarettes, but he couldn't see anyone's features.

He didn't think too much about it. Before he knew it, he was running toward the back end of the wagon, which was hidden from view from the store by the gas pump. As he approached, knowing what he was about to do, all he could think of was watching Damien voluntarily get into that car the previous day. Landon imagined everyone he knew shouting at him not to jump into the car, knowing he was accepting the same fate, whatever it may be, that his friends fell victim to.

Having hurled himself into the back of the wagon, he rolled onto a jumbled mess of junk, some of it soft and crinkling under him, while other objects jabbed him in the ribs and gouged his back. He flailed about to gain control of the insane situation he had just gotten himself into and take cover. He was convinced the commotion he was making in the back of the wagon would certainly draw attention from anyone around, but the other vehicles at the pump had pulled away except for the one pickup truck that still sat on the right, blocking the view of the wagon from the store. The driver of that truck had already pumped his gas and sat in the idling truck. A second later, Landon heard him pull away and knew he was in full view of the windows of the store. Landon wriggled and squirmed to burrow down in the pile of junk until he was satisfied that he was completely hidden from view.

Landon was a pro at hide and seek. He knew he had to remain perfectly still and breathe as lightly as possible so that his ribcage expanding and deflating wouldn't create motion in the mess covering him. He had no idea of what his next move would be once they arrived at their destination.

Then he heard the heavy car door creak open. The wagon was jostled as the driver settled into it, and Landon could tell by the amount of movement of the large vehicle that the driver was of considerable weight. The door slammed shut with a dull clunk.

Landon began to panic at what he had just gotten himself into. He had just willingly volunteered to be this man's next victim. How delightful for this kidnapper to have simply pulled up to a gas station and have a kid run up and jump into his vehicle.

Landon determined it was a man driving the car when he cleared his throat and hacked something up. He heard him spit out the window as the wagon shifted into gear and began smoothly pulling away from the gas pump.

"Stupid idiot," the man grumbled angrily as the car jolted.

A wave of fear swept through Landon, sensing that the man had suddenly just realized he had a stowaway in his vehicle. Landon remained quiet, perfectly still, knowing he had been discovered.

"Didn't see you there," the man remarked obnoxiously from up front.

Landon's heart pounded. He winced. He wondered if the kidnapper had seen him jump in from the window when he was inside the convenience store. Landon didn't think he would have had a view from the store windows, but perhaps he was on his way out. Maybe he was in a different section of the store and saw him from there. He wondered if part of his body was protruding enough to be noticed in the rearview mirror, but he seemed to be low in the car, tucked behind the backseat against the floor. He couldn't lift his head to peek. Maybe part of his body was protruding obviously, making him like an ostrich with its head stuck in the sand. Perhaps this frighteningly calm man had seen him from the second he got in the car and decided devilishly to go about his business as if nothing was wrong and continue on his journey.

As the car began to move, Landon was sure that the man knew he was there. He kept perfectly still, though, hoping to convince him that he wasn't there, that perhaps he had imagined it.

"Where do you think you're going?" the man suddenly asked him.

Landon stopped breathing. His heart slammed against his ribcage and he was ready to throw everything off him and jump from the back window.

"Learn how to drive, moron!" the man yelled as the wagon lunged forward, making the rear tires squeal.

Landon let out a slow sigh of relief as he realized the man was reacting to other drivers, not to him. They hit a big bump and everything in the trunk launched in the air for a moment, including him, landing with a clunk and knocking the breath out of him. Landon was so startled that a yelp came out of him and he feared it was loud enough to be heard from the front seat. He felt the vehicle slow a little. He was certain he had been heard, and swore the driver was now pulling the car off to the side of the road, or worse yet, he was taking him to a remote place where he could deal with him as he pleased with no witnesses around. The ultimate terror was realizing that he was completely at the mercy of the man behind the wheel. When he had seen the car and jumped in, it was a feeling of power for him, taking matters into his own hands and doing something courageous to help his friends. Now it was starting to seem incredibly foolish not only to have put his own life on the line but also to have caused yet another missing child in the community, another soul lost to the monster everyone feared.

He thought about suddenly uncovering himself and making a leap for the back window he had entered through, but he knew it would be difficult to slip out of— and who knew what was behind him. They were moving at a good clip and he could get injured or killed bailing out of the back, if he even made it through the window before being noticed.

As much as he wanted to help his friends, the anger had given way to pure fear. He just wanted to be back at home again with his parents, snug under a blanket watching afternoon cartoons. He didn't know why he had gotten in the car. He didn't think he could make it to the window without being seen in the rearview mirror, especially if the driver already knew he was there. Even if he didn't know he was there, Landon doubted that he could make it without being seen and heard—and if he was seen or heard, he knew that the back window was electric and the driver could close it from the front seat.

The noise in the back suddenly began quieting down. He froze, petrified. He realized the pane of glass of the rear window must have been sliding up to meet with the top of the window frame. It sealed shut. His heart dropped. His only potential escape route, as unlikely as it was that he would use it, was gone. He was trapped, completely. Even when the car stopped at its final destination—*his* final destination—he would not be able to escape through the back. He would have to open a door. If the vehicle was locked when the driver exited, he would have to unlock it before he could even leave the car.

He could feel the wagon slowing down. He knew they had traveled a long way from town—and from help. What would the man do once he was discovered? He prayed that the man would just leave the car and go into his house. Then, alone in the car, Landon could open a door and escape, taking note of the location, the house number maybe, anything to tell to the police about where, most likely, the two missing children were being held. He had found the den of the kidnapper. He had found the monster's lair.

The wagon slowed to a crawl and he felt it turn. The ride became extremely choppy, jostling him and all the junk in the back. He felt as though he was being slid toward the tailgate of the car, as if it was traveling at a significant angle upward. He stabilized himself by spreading his arms and leg wider on the floor to keep himself from rolling over completely.

The ascent stopped and the wagon leveled out. It bounced a few more times before the brakes squeaked and the motion came to a stop. He heard it shift into park with a slight increase in the tone of the idle, and then the engine cut out.

Landon heard the front door pop open. He felt the cool rush of air from outside make its way back to him.

Landon's heart was in his throat, making his breathing quiver.

The door slammed shut up front with a creak and a bang.

He was breathing so hard and heavy and was in such a panic that he couldn't control it anymore. His entire body was shaking.

Landon heard the footsteps crunch in the leaves, heavy and spaced far apart. They were moving along the side of the vehicle toward the back. He could hear them pass by where his head rested against the carpet of the wheel well.

His eyes bulged wide in terror. His right fist clenched around the knife handle so tightly his fingers were going numb and tingly. They were sweating intensely. His small Swiss Army knife was his only defense, and he prayed he had the nerve to actually use it. The knife had made him feel so powerful before, like such a man, a savage hunter who could take on anyone, but now he realized how powerless he was. He was nowhere near a man. It was just a little knife with a little blade that he didn't have the nerve to use; even if he did, it probably wouldn't do much damage.

The footsteps halted behind the back hatch.

The latch of the hatchback clicked.

Every muscle in Landon's body contracted. Adrenaline surged through his veins and made him ready to explode.

The back hatch lifted open.

He heard a few items fall out and clatter to the ground, banging on each other and the car as they spilled out of the overfilled wagon.

The freezing air rushed in all around Landon. He was already trembling. He felt like a wild animal caught in a trap, willing to do anything to escape, becoming totally focused on fighting for its survival.

He did everything he could not to move, not to flinch, not to make a sound. He was horrified that he was already in plain view, although nothing seemed to be happening. There was no sound, just cool air rushing in.

He felt something being moved by his feet.

He heard the man grunt in frustration as things shifted around the back. Something else hit the ground, tumbling out.

The man swore to himself.

Landon felt the blanket being tugged on, pulled off his hair, and beginning to slide off his face. He remained perfectly still. This was it.

The blanket was suddenly yanked off his lower half and he felt the sudden bitter cold on his ankles.

He knew his feet were now in plain view, totally exposed.

The motion suddenly stopped.

All went silent.

Landon held his breath. He was ready to explode into action.

There was no further sound. Nothing moved.

Then the tarp was suddenly ripped off him in one quick and final tug, sending random items slamming against the side of the wagon and, in one instant, fully exposing him.

Landon flipped himself over and sprung onto his hands and knees in a defensive position, like a cat ready to fight, and saw the man standing in front of him, hunched over and peering into the trunk of his wagon. He was a large, beastly man with a full beard. He looked like a lumberjack with enormous wide shoulders and big dark eyes, and he had an absolutely blank stare on his face that shot terror through Landon's body. He stood perfectly still as a statue, ready to strike, looking down on the prey he had snared, the defenseless little person who had dared intrude upon his property and follow him in a desperate attempt to bring him to justice. All Landon could see was anger and rage in the man's eyes despite his total lack of expression, and it was the most frightening face he had ever seen.

Landon felt the knife in a death grip in his right hand, which quickly raised up behind his head, as he simultaneously pushed his right sneaker against the back of the seat and launched himself at the man with everything he had, knowing it might be the last thing he ever did.

Completely stunned by this unexpected aggression, the man flinched in surprise with his hands up as the boy came at him with the knife pointed at his face in his outstretched hand.

Landon made contact with something. His right hand and the knife were deflected upward, missing the man completely, leaving him to impact the man's body without causing any damage to him.

He felt the man's large arms wrap around him like two pythons tightening on their prey, until they squeezed him so tightly he could barely breathe, picking him up and turning away from the open hatch of the wagon. The man then stood upright to his full height, which must have been at least six and a half feet, raising Landon high off the ground.

Landon tried to raise the knife again, to wind it back behind his head, to gain some leverage so that he could make another attempt at lashing at the man, anything to do damage and make him put him down, but the angle was wrong and Landon could only slice at the air around them.

Landon felt himself being whipped in one direction and then back to the other quickly in a jerking motion. There was a solid smack on his back and he realized that he had been thrown to the ground, making all of his limbs spread out. He felt the sharp impact of a huge boot tip hitting his hand. He felt the pain in his fingers from the hard, heavy boot attached to the giant man. The knife was gone from his fingers, launched far off into the grass.

"*What do you think you're doing!*" the man bellowed down at him in the grass, his giant figure looming over him.

Landon swung himself onto his side and pushed himself to his feet, stumbling a few steps. He was almost up before he was knocked down again by his legs being swept out from under him.

"Hey!" the man shouted at him. "Where do you think you're going?"

Before Landon had hit the ground, he was already gaining his footing again, trying desperately to get away, but all the while knowing he could never outrun this powerful predator.

The man snagged him by the back of his jacket and picked him up off the ground, pulling him backward and making him tumble back to the ground again.

Landon felt the big hands grab him. He was lifted up over six feet in the air. His legs kicked and his arms swung at nothing as he was flung over the shoulder of the giant man like a sack of potatoes. He screamed at the top of his lungs and hollered, but it didn't do any good. He heard the man struggle with the load on his shoulders to unlatch a door.

He felt a wave of heat slap him in the face with the smell of a fireplace smoking. It smelled like soup.

The man put him down.

Landon instantly ran for the door, but the man snagged him again by the jacket and pulled him down onto the wooden planks of the cottage.

"Where do you think you're going? Huh?" the man yelled down at him.

Landon scampered to his feet and struggled pathetically against the brute force holding him.

"You want to tell me just what you were doing in my trunk, kid?" the man asked as he was jerked about by the boy, struggling to maintain a hold on him. "Knock it off!" the man screamed at Landon, his voice booming through the house.

Landon could feel the deep sound waves beat through his insides like a loud bass sound booming from a speaker.

The man picked him up again, clearly losing his cool and growing frustrated with his struggling, then folded Landon's arms over each other and plopped him down into a wooden chair in the kitchen. He hunched over to get down to his level and glared at him with angry bloodshot eyes, puffing out putrid clouds of breath in his face.

"Why did you do that do me?" the man asked with confusion and frustration. "Why did you hide in my car and attack me like that?"

"Let me go!" Landon shouted as he struggled hopelessly against the man's burly arms.

"You're not going anywhere kid until you give me some answers."

"Landon?" came a small voice from the hallway.

They both fell silent and Landon stopped his struggling.

The large man turned to face the hallway and said, "You, go back to your room!"

"Who is that?" the child's voice asked.

"I said to go back to your room!"

"Landon? Is that you?" the young voice asked.

Landon saw Damien appear slowly, scared, in the doorway, wearing a pair of sweatpants and a shirt with a skateboarder on it.

The man looked at Landon. Then he looked back at Damien. "You know this boy?"

"Yeah," Damien answered.

"How do you know him?"

"He's in my grade. He's my friend Landon, Dad. Don't hurt him, please."

The man took a few deep breaths and sighed heavily. He rolled his eyes.

Landon felt the grip on his arms loosen. The man unclenched his fingers, releasing his arms, then lowered his arms to his sides and stood up straight, looking down at the boy in his chair.

Landon rubbed his arms, which were red from the man's fingers squeezing against his struggling.

Damien's father bellowed down at him, "Would you like to explain just what you were doing in my car, then?"

"I was looking for Emily," Landon said, still frightened, "and Damien. I was trying to find them."

Damien's father sighed and looked at the floor. "Emily Rose, right? That's the little girl who disappeared from town a couple weeks ago?"

"It was last week," Landon said.

"You thought she was here? With me?" Damien's father asked softly, confused.

"I didn't know who you were," Landon explained. "I didn't know you were Damien's dad. I just saw him get in your car the other day at school, and then everybody said he was missing. I'm sorry.... I had no idea that he was just with his dad. He never mentioned anything about you or about going to stay with you."

"That's because he's not supposed to be here with me. His mom has sole custody of him. That means she gets him all the time and I have absolutely no say in what goes on in his life or in that house of hers. I have no control over what guy she's bringing around my kid—and who she has living with her. Did you happen to notice all those bruises and cuts on Damien's face?"

Landon nodded.

"Those aren't from a skateboarding accident. They're from that loser his mother's shacking up with. He's the one who's doing it. I've done everything I can to put a stop to it, but the problem is his mother. She defends the loser who's hitting my kid and doing drugs in his face. She lies and tells the cops that he fell. She makes him lie to the cops and to his teachers too. They all lie about the beatings and the drug abuse going on in that house. And the few times I stepped in, I almost went to jail myself, just for trying to protect my little boy. Nobody hits my boy. That's why I picked him up and took him here."

Landon looked at Damien in dismay, having a hard time believing his friend had concealed all this from him for so long. "The whole town thinks that he's missing, though."

"They can think that all they want," Damien's father responded angrily. "I don't care what they think, as long as my boy is safe and out of harm's way."

"The police are out looking for him everywhere," Landon added.

"Let them arrest me. They can throw me in jail. It wouldn't be the first time. You need to understand something, Landon. I will never sit back and let my son be abused by anyone. Nothing else matters to me. I'm sure your father would do the same for you if you were in Damien's situation." He looked over at his son, who was peeking around the wall despite his father's warning. "Okay. I'll drive you home. Damien, get your coat on. You're coming too."

"Wait a minute..." Damien said to his father, entering the kitchen. "I need to talk to Landon for a second."

"Okay. Just get your coat on and come out when you're ready," Damien's father said to him as he pushed his way through the kitchen door outside, making some bells on the door jingle.

Damien grabbed his boots by the door and sat in one of the wood chairs to put them on. "I'm going to be going away for a while," he told Landon.

Landon's heart sank. He knew he was about to lose the only friend he had left. "Where are you going?"

"I'm not supposed to say," he said as though he was well aware of the consequences of his father's actions, "but I want to tell you something about Emily. She made me swear on my life to never tell anyone." He paused, seeming uncertain if telling Landon was the right thing to do. "I know where her diary is. I gave her my word that I would take that secret to my grave. She trusted me, but I've been thinking about it ever since she disappeared, that maybe she wrote something in it.... Maybe she saw something unusual or met someone new.... Maybe she had plans to run away from home, or she knew that someone was after her. I was going to get it myself after we found Chester in the woods. I was going to find it and read it to see if there was anything that could help find her. I know she would forgive me for telling if it meant finding her alive."

Landon was filled with newfound hope and became excited by the possibility of a new lead. "Where is it?"

"It's in the yellow playhouse way in the back behind their house. Do you know what I'm talking about?"

"Yeah. I've been in it." Landon was very familiar with the "play house" that was not only larger but more lavishly decorated that his family's home. The only difference was that the ceilings were lower than a real house and the furniture was child-sized.

"It's in the dish cabinet in the dining room, inside the little drawer near the bottom of it."

Landon thanked his friend with his eyes.

"Just be careful," Damien said to him as they headed out the door to the old brown station wagon that had previously haunted him.

23

The next day, on his way home from school, Landon slowed as he passed by the Rose mansion. He was surprised to find all the gates to the property closed because often the gate to the front entry was left open during the day.

He moved toward the gate that had swung open the last time he stopped in front of the house, when Winston frightened him. He reached out toward the gate. He felt its cold, black, painted steel on his palm as his fingers wrapped around one of its bars. He nonchalantly gave it a gentle tug. Nothing happened. He pulled it a little harder, making the entire gate shake.

Suddenly there was a strange sensation of being caught doing something he wasn't supposed to. His eyes darted to the mansion and instantly focused on the second to last window on the left side of the house on the second story—Emily's room.

There was a figure standing within its glass, holding the curtain open to peer out—watching Landon pull on the gate to gain access to the property.

Landon gasped. He couldn't make out any features of the figure, but he could see the outline of a person. The curtains moved slightly.

Landon quickly looked away and hurried down the sidewalk, pretending to go about his business, too afraid to look back.

Landon began pummeling his fists into his skull. He grabbed his hair and the skin underneath and squeezed in a ridiculous display of lost temper. He had finally reached a breaking point, knowing it was there and he couldn't get it; all he had to do to end this nightmare was remember what happened to him.

"*Landon*," his mother's voice said from the doorway with great alarm.

He swiveled quickly, stunned, dropping his hands from his head and letting them hang innocently at his side.

"What in the world were you doing to yourself?" Her face scrunched in an equal mixture of concern and fright.

Landon looked at her blankly. He was startled, having had no idea anyone had been watching him and he began to think how that must have looked to his mother.

"There's red marks on you.... Why were you doing that?" she asked, coming toward him in the room but stopping a few feet away, still stunned and a little scared by his strange behavior.

"I was trying to remember," he answered softly.

"Is that what you did to the back of your head the other night? Did you hit yourself with something then, too?"

"No...."

"Have you hit anyone else with anything?"

"No, Mom.... I was just mad at myself. I was mad because I couldn't remember what I did."

She had tears in her eyes as if it was the hardest thing she had ever done. "I didn't want to do this. I thought there was some other way. I thought they would have found her by now, or found...something." She was trying to maintain her composure and be brave. "I'm going to take you to see a doctor tomorrow. One that will talk to you and ask you lots of questions. I think it's what needs to be done for everyone...and for you."

24

Chester awoke suddenly from a sound sleep. He lifted his head from the filthy old mattress he had found in town next to a garbage can. He inhaled deeply; there was a thick odor in the air that smelled like a wood stove burning. He had put out the fire in his fireplace before he came to bed.

His groggy senses were struggling to get his attention and warn him of danger. He threw his musty blanket off and sprang from his mattress. He could see the room clearly, as if it was morning, but he knew it wasn't. There was an orange glow to his home that was quickly intensifying, and when he felt the heat, he knew he had to get out.

He staggered in different directions a few times in a panic, his body reacting faster than his mind. He felt the need to gather his only possessions in the world and save them. He saw the shelves full of books ignite. The fire was spreading rampantly and he knew he had very little time.

He grabbed his stuffed dog off the bed he had made for him.

He snagged his backpack by a strap and flung it over his shoulder. The fire was spreading too quickly. He looked around desperately to see what else he could salvage, but he could see one of his escape routes already engulfed in flames. The other way out, through the foundation of the mill, was in danger of catching fire soon as well and becoming impassable.

Chester bolted toward the doorway. A beam fell across his path as he went, tripping him and sending him to the floor.

Smoke was filling the mill with the flames, turning his home into a fiery vision of hell.

The heat was burning his face, forcing him to squint his eyes. It became incredibly difficult to breathe, and it was only because of lying on the ground, below the heat and smoke, that he was able to inhale the breath he so desperately needed.

He scrambled on his hands and knees toward the entrance, clinging to Chip. The fire was nearing his last exit and he scrambled desperately, sensing his time was limited. In his scuffle, Chip came out of his hand somehow and was left behind on the wood planks. A flaming beam crashed down right behind Chester, missing his legs by inches. He stumbled away, stunned by the near miss but still desperately clinging to life. His heart dropped as he realized Chip was under the burning beam, which he actually, for one moment, considered lifting off him. Even if he could lift the weight, the flames would eat him alive. He yelled out in agony, realizing it was too late. He had to let Chip go. The flames were growing. He didn't think he would make it out alive, but he had to try. He launched himself through the burning entrance to the basement of the structure and he felt the flames sear his arms and burn off his eyebrows and eyelashes, but he kept going.

He ran outside into the cool autumn night and then buckled over, coughing and hacking. There was nothing he could do except helplessly watch his home burn to the ground until the fire had consumed all he had to cling to in this world. Once again, life as he knew it had been stolen from him.

25

"It's nice to meet you, Landon. My name is Doctor Jacobs and I'm a clinical psychologist," said the man seated in the leather armchair across from Landon.

The doctor was very lanky with big ears that extended well beyond normal, making it difficult for Landon to pay attention to what he was saying. He felt terrible for staring and even thinking mocking thoughts; the doctor must have endured a great deal of ridicule growing up. This man had done nothing wrong to him and was taking him seriously. At the same time, Landon couldn't help but think that with his perfectly trimmed beard and dark beady eyes the doctor looked just like the gnome from the travel commercials on TV.

"I want to thank you for agreeing to meet me today," Doctor Jacobs continued. "I understand you've been through a lot, and I want you to know that nothing we do here today is meant to make you more uncomfortable. We don't want to do anything that is going to upset you or cause you harm. I simply want to help you find answers and, hopefully, those answers can help the police locate Emily." He looked over at Mrs. Daniels, who appeared mortified. "Mrs. Daniels, are you feeling all right?"

She shook her head no. "I don't like anything about this," she said softly, knowing she had no choice.

"There's nothing to be afraid of," the doctor reassured her. "I'm only here to talk to Landon."

"I'm petrified of what is going to come out," Mrs. Daniels admitted. "I know my son. I love him and know he would never hurt anyone else. But what if he says something that didn't really happen? What if his mind has been influenced by all that's going on...? What if he creates some fantasy in his head because he feels responsible?"

"You mean a false memory?" Doctor Jacobs suggested.

"Yes. What if he says something that didn't even happen because he created a false memory?"

"Mrs. Daniels, I understand your concern completely. I assure you we are taking that into consideration. We're not looking to jump to any conclusions. We're not looking for our villain, here. We hope that by potentially accessing those memories that are just beneath the surface and not too far gone to recover that we may very well be able to get some clue, some image, some memory of her whereabouts or some piece of information that will allow us to eventually find her. We need to know the truth."

There was a long pause from his mother. Tears were forming in her eyes. She said quietly, almost ashamed, "I'm afraid of the truth."

Carter turned to Landon and looked him in the eyes. He could see that he was shaken up by the way his mother was talking, her doubt in him, and her concern was beginning to wear on him and gnaw at his nerves. "Landon," Carter said to him. "Don't you want to know the truth?"

Landon paused for a moment, bothered and afraid. Then he nodded, clearly, bravely. "I want to know what happened to her."

Carter glanced over at his mother, who lowered her head, giving in. He nodded and closed his eyes. "Good. Let's begin then."

They went through a series of what seemed like over a hundred questions, some of which Landon had no idea why he asked. He concluded that the doctor was evaluating his mental clarity and was more interested in *how* he answered than what he *said*.

When the testing was over, Doctor Jacobs said, after a long break, "You appear to be a perfectly normal functioning individual. Despite that nasty bump on your head, everything seems to be working properly. Your cognitive functions are intact. Your logic and reason are sharp and accurate. Your brain is working as it should be," Doctor Jacobs said with a positive and factual tone.

"Then why can't I remember?" Landon asked with some frustration in his voice.

The sides of Doctor Jacobs' mouth dropped slightly and he inhaled a deep breath through his nose, making his nostrils flare. "There are two types of memory lapses you may have suffered. It is possible that the memory loss you're experiencing is a result of what is called organic amnesia, which results from direct damage to the brain caused by head injury, physical trauma or disease. The second possibility is something we call dissociative amnesia, which is caused by a traumatic event, where something so disturbing occurs that your brain chooses to forget the event rather than deal with the stress. Dissociative amnesia occurs when a person blocks out certain pieces of time, leaving him or her unable to remember important personal information. With this disorder, the degree of memory loss goes beyond normal forgetfulness and includes gaps in memory for long periods of time or of memories involving the traumatic event. It is an inability to recall information, usually about stressful or traumatic events in persons' lives, such as a violent attack or disaster. The memory is stored in long-term memory, but access to it is impaired because of psychological defense mechanisms. People with this affliction retain the capacity to learn new information and there may be some later partial or complete recovery of memory. Do you have any questions about what I just said?"

Landon stared at him blankly, overwhelmed and slightly embarrassed that he had no idea what the doctor had said. He nodded his head no.

"Now, Landon, I want you to get in a comfortable position. You can even lie down on the couch if you want." He motioned to the leather sofa to the right of his chair. "Or, if you're more comfortable, just stay in the chair where you are. The important thing is that you're at ease with your environment and that you feel safe."

Landon looked around at his mother and then at Carter, who looked on expressionless. "I'll stay in the chair."

"Good." Doctor Jacobs gave him a warm, reassuring smile. "Now, I want you to get as relaxed in the chair as possible. Close your eyes. Slump down in that soft chair and imagine yourself sinking gently into it and its softness enveloping you like a cloud. Starting with your forehead, begin relaxing every muscle in your body. Release the tension in your forehead and focus on letting those muscles relax. Now, like a beam of relaxing light is slowly moving down your body and through you, relax your neck against the chair. Relax your arms from your elbows right down to your hands, down to your fingers and out to your fingertips. There is no need to move them anymore."

As Landon remained motionless, a strange sensation of numbness came over him. He focused only on the doctor's soothing commands and making his weary, overstressed body calm down.

"Now, that ray of light is moving down through your abdomen," Doctor Jacobs continued. "Feel it warm you and relax you as it passes over your stomach and down to your legs. Relax your thighs, your knees, then all the way down to your feet, and then feel the heat radiate out to your toes. Remain perfectly still. Take a deep, slow breath. Now, while you exhale, visualize the negativity and tension escaping in the form of a dark cloud. Now, with that dark cloud of tension gone, a clear and bright atmosphere full of energy will encompass you. You are perfectly safe here. Nothing you think or feel can harm you.

Now, I want you to visualize standing at the top of a flight of ten stairs. Gently take your first step down and know that everything is fine. Focus on the stairs beneath you. Now, descend the remaining nine stairs with me and count each one aloud."

Together, they began counting down from nine. Landon could see a beautiful, peaceful world beneath him, as the doctor had instructed. He felt more relaxed than he ever had and felt very disconnected from his life and his problems. He was in a different world where he could escape his life for a while.

"As you reach the fifth step, visualize yourself stepping into a clean and pure oasis of water. With each additional step down, you find yourself getting deeper and deeper into the water, washing away any doubts you have.

You are now at the bottom of the staircase and the warm water is up to your neck, giving you a floating sensation. This floating sensation is the only thing you can feel.

While you are floating, I want you to think back to last week, this most recent Halloween. You can remember getting ready to go out with your friends, Damien and Emily. I want you to think about all the things you did to get ready in anticipation of meeting your friends. Think about the excitement you felt, the feeling of not being able to wait to go out with them. Remember dressing up in your costume before you left your house."

Landon remembered looking in the mirror at himself in the Yankees uniform and his mother taking pictures, one too many for his pleasure. He rolled his eyes at her to stop. The flash was blinding him and he tripped over the jacket he had tossed on the floor after school. His mother told him that's why he should remember to take a second and put things where they belong.

"Think about trick-or-treating with them, the houses you went to, what was said and what you were feeling as you walked."

Landon could hear the voices of other kids talking, laughing and shouting as they scared each other in the crisp autumn air. Kids were everywhere. The smell of wood stoves burning mixed with fallen leaves and the scent of cinnamon and apples at his house. He remembered feeling nervous but having such a great sense of enjoyment. There were so many houses and so little time. They needed to regroup and plan their candy heist of the neighborhood.

"Remember what you were feeling when Damien left you because Emily held your hand, when she took *your hand*. Remember what you felt for your friend and the feelings you were having toward Emily. Remember her face, the way she smiled at you, the things she said and what you were talking about."

Landon saw vivid flashes of Emily's face like single frames in an old movie, images that appeared and disappeared just as fast, leaving a split-second impression for the mind to process and try to grasp. He felt his heart rate accelerate as the memories emerged from the deep and he saw her, he heard her voice, her giggle. They were talking, but there were no words, just voices, sounds. She was there with him.

"Remember where you headed that night while trick-or-treating, as things got later. Think about where you went, what you were going to do. Think about the last time you saw her, the last moments you spent with her, what she was feeling, what you were thinking, things she said. I want you to remember what she was doing. I want you to picture her face clearly in your mind; remember what she looked like and what was happening between the two of you. Remember her expressions, her mood and what she was saying to you. Remember what she was telling you the last time you saw her. Remember where you were, and who you were with."

Landon was elated that he could actually picture her that night, even if only in flashes. It was the first glimpse he had into that fateful night, despite having lived it. The bits of information and missing time were inside his mind after all and could be accessed, even if through great difficulty. Then, he heard the thunder. A horrible feeling swept over him. "*No*," he protested aloud in the doctor's office.

"You are perfectly safe, Landon," Doctor Jacobs soothed him. "Do not be afraid. Open your mind and allow the memories back in."

They were up so high together, much higher than they should have been. He heard her scream over the thunder and then it faded into the darkness. There was a flash of her face, and he could see the pure terror in her eyes. Her mouth hung open as she screamed at him through scattered, distorted sound waves.

Landon began convulsing in his chair and yelled fragments of words that were unrecognizable to his mother and Doctor Jacobs.

"Let the memories come back," Doctor Jacobs instructed him forcefully. "Let them in, Landon. *Let them in*."

The white light was upon him—the thunder boomed—the terrified expression on her face—she was petrified of him, the horrible image burned into his mind, she was scared to death of *him*. She screamed at him and it echoed through his room at home—his closet door was opening—the beam of light became wider and wider from the door as it opened, and he yelled for them to stop, to leave him alone. The light glared, and thunder shook the house—but they were coming in, it was too late—Emily screamed to him, she screamed for her life, she screamed as if she was certain she was about to die.

Landon jolted back to reality, snapping his eyes open and shooting upright in the chair, practically launching himself off it hollering out in sheer terror.

"Landon! Landon!" Doctor Jacobs grabbed his shoulders.

"I saw her—I saw Emily," Landon blurted out with his eyes bulging, gasping for breath.

"Where did you see her?" Doctor Jacobs leaned forward in his seat.

"On the bridge—on the train bridge over the gorge—I saw her there screaming.... She was screaming at me," he said with tears in his eyes. "She was so scared...."

"What were you doing there with her?" Doctor Jacobs asked intensely.

Landon shook his head in a daze trying to get control of himself. "They got in."

"That's enough," his mother said as she rushed to his side and embraced him. "He's had enough."

"Who got in?" Doctor Jacobs rushed forward to Landon before he lost him. "Who, Landon?"

Landon's eyes glazed over. His face went pale. Before his eyes rolled back in his head, and he collapsed in the chair, he muttered, "*The paper dolls.*"

26

Carter had assembled the police search team, including the dogs, to pick up any possible scents. Now that they at least had some direction, he knew it was the best lead they had so far, even though it was far from solid. He worried that Landon had been spooked into seeing what he *dreaded* happened to Emily, not what *really* happened, based on the nightmares he had been having—just as his mother had feared.

The water down in the middle of the gorge was not deep, but Carter knew it would wash away any evidence that may have landed in it. The first pass through the gorge proved fruitless, as did the second. On the third pass, the dogs indicated a strong indication of a scent. Carter approached and saw with his own eyes what they were excited about. He could see some dark maroon dried blood on the leaves of a sapling and a rock nearby. He looked around but didn't see any more.

Then he looked up. Shielding his eyes from the glaring afternoon sun, he could see they were directly under the middle of the railroad bridge far overhead. He estimated it had to be at least one hundred fifty feet, maybe one hundred sixty.

Had the blood come from a body falling over the side of the bridge? Did only the blood due to an injury fall from the bridge such as the one that Landon suffered while Emily remained on the bridge? There wasn't a consistent enough blood pattern to differentiate a splatter from an impact or blood fallen from above. If the blood came from above, there would also be a splatter effect from it hitting the rock.

If she had fallen from the bridge, then where was the body? There was simply no way she could have survived a fall from that height. Could the boy have dragged her body away by himself? Did wild animals come and scavenge the body? Wolves and coyotes were common in the area. Carter had to consider it, as much as it churned his stomach.

"Have them pick up a scent from the blood here," Carter said to the officer handling the dogs.

"We already have a scent from the clothes Mr. Rose gave us," the officer contended.

Carter shook his head. "Use the blood," he ordered.

They would begin searching the surrounding woods with the dogs. The sooner the better, before it rained and washed away scents and blood splatter. Carter himself would examine the bridge above. He walked it back and forth slowly with the dogs, their noses remaining glued to the dirt on the bridge as they sniffed and snorted. From their interest, it was clear that the blood came from a person who had indeed walked on that bridge, but no additional evidence was discovered.

The condition of the bridge was shockingly poor, a perfect example of neglected infrastructure in this country. It was rusting, crumbling, and sections of its floor were gone. Carter was startled by how unsafe he felt walking across it, but then again it was not intended to be a footbridge. He assumed the integrity of the bridge was intact since it had no trouble supporting the heavy trains that frequently traveled over it.

Carter could clearly see mountains fifteen miles away. He leaned over the rail to gaze down at where he had found the blood and was instantly sweating. The height was dizzying, and the thought of anyone falling from the bridge into the gorge below was enough to panic him. He had to step back, dizzy and afraid to move. The wind whipped through the gorge, puffing his coat and tossing his hair. He wondered if this was it—if this was the exact location where Emily Rose met her fate.

27

Landon didn't care what his parents said. Emily had been gone too long, and he was too close to remembering. He was afraid of the truth, and he knew that now. He knew he was there that night with her, when something happened to Emily—and he *saw* what happened. Maybe that's why he blocked it out, because it was so shocking and disturbing that he suffered a mental lapse. He would have remembered in the doctor's office if he hadn't withdrawn out of fear and stopped the procedure, but it was time to confront the truth.

He waited until his parents were asleep. He watched the shadows of the branches dancing on his shades, images from the full moon's glow. He had left the shade up on the one window that overlooked the roof of the garage. It wasn't the first time he had snuck out of the house.

Landon's heart pounded as he listened to his own breaths in the dark. His parents were sound asleep. They were exhausted. There was nothing he'd rather do than lie in bed and go to sleep, but his mind would not let him rest. There was something that needed to be done, although he still was not sure what that was.

He gently peeled the covers off his upper body and then kicked them off his legs. He sat straight up in bed slowly and waited for a moment, making sure he still couldn't hear anyone awake. Satisfied that his parents were asleep, he crawled across the covers, over his bed, to the edge of it closest to the window with the shade up. He cautiously probed down with his right foot for the wood floor, which he felt, then gradually lowered his full weight onto the floor and planted his left foot as well, met with the usual unavoidable creaks.

He reached down and grabbed the jacket he had placed on the floor in preparation, hidden under the corner of his bed by the wall. He slipped it on quietly and zipped it up.

He put his hands on either side of the window frame and gently, carefully pushed up, trying hard to avoid it suddenly giving way and crackling open as it often did. It slid up nearly silently and the brisk air from outside instantly chilled him, rushing through the opening in the window and cooling his feet. He put on his shoes and tied them quickly. He lifted one leg and swung it out the window and over the sill. He leaned forward so his weight was on his abdomen and lowered his left leg, outside, until he felt the roof with the toe of his shoe. He put his weight onto his left shoe and hung onto the sill as he lowered his right leg as well. Now, standing on the soft roof shingles, he reached up and pulled the window shut as stealthily as he had opened it. He looked around. It looked like he was so much higher up than he was, especially in the dark.

He practiced it mentally a few times before taking a running leap at the small tree growing next to the roof about six feet away. It was a much harsher impact than he had intended, and he slammed into the narrow trunk, shaking the whole tree and sending its dead orange leaves sailing to the ground. He practically fell down the tree, grabbing its thin branches that barely supported his weight and stumbling down until he let go completely and dropped to the ground with a dull thud. The impact made him bend his knees and drop to his butt, nearly toppling backward into the grass and dried leaves under him.

He moved quickly through the woods with his flashlight, barely able to see in front of him. A horrible feeling of fear and panic overtook him as he realized that he didn't know exactly where he was. He had been following the path he was most familiar with, but the darkness played tricks with his vision and distorted distances. He became paranoid that he was heading into the middle of nowhere, all alone in the darkness, and worried about what would happen if his flashlight battery died. Everything inside him told him this was a bad idea, that he didn't want to know, but there was the one nagging feeling inside of him, guiding him forward against his will, telling him he *had* to know, whether he wanted to or not, what happened that night to Emily.

He remembered the feeling of her hand on his when she took it, pulling him across the street. He remembered how beautiful and magical it felt when she kept holding onto it even after she had led him across, making it clear to him, for the first time ever, that he was something more significant than just a friend to her. It made him feel grown up, like a man, that she would even be interested in him with all the boys after her. She could have her pick of them and he had no idea why she would be interested in him, but he was hardly about to argue since it was the greatest thing he had ever experienced, and it promised many more amazing new experiences to come.

He remembered her costume, how it tantalized him and made him stare much longer than he knew he should have. Her outfit was more revealing than he had expected, and it made her look so pretty, with her beads on and her makeup, which she normally didn't wear. How ridiculous it was that a costume made her suddenly look so attractive; he begin to realize that maybe it was because the costume allowed him to see her in a totally different light, not just as the tomboy he was friends with. She was suddenly very feminine, delicate and beautiful, a new person he had not met before, who was intriguing and exciting. He felt nervous for the first time around her, awkward and timid. He was more courteous to her than usual, allowing her to go first; rather than be freaked out by it, she responded well. She seemed to like his new role as well and welcomed his newfound manliness.

As he continued to stumble through the woods, he remembered how bad he felt for Damien when Emily first held his hand; he had seemingly won without even trying. It was very bittersweet for him; he felt terrible for his friend's hurt feelings, but this newly discovered euphoria was clouding over his negative emotions like a powerful drug. He had to struggle to feel the bad feelings he knew he should feel, and he followed after his friend when he turned from them to head back home, sulking. Emily yelled after him, telling him to stop, although she didn't seem quite as concerned about their friend as he was. He was heartbroken that he had hurt Damien so much, but it was almost as if he was moving onto a different phase of his life, one beyond the imaginary adventures, cardboard box battleships and plastic battling military forces. Something had happened in that one moment that made him realize he was growing up and things were changing. The second she had taken his hand, it was as if all of his priorities in life had shifted and they would never be the same.

As Damien faded into the darkness holding his head in his hands, defeated, his spirit broken, Landon knew he had to let him go. There was nothing he could say or do, since the damage was already done. He hoped his friend would forgive him one day.

Landon stopped in the middle of the woods, startled. He quickly spun around. His feet stomped in the brush, snapping twigs and crushing dried leaves. He shined his flashlight back and forth behind him, crouched, ready to confront whoever or whatever had been following him. He was losing it. It was just like walking home from school with the constant feeling of being watched and followed. There was no one there, as far as he could tell, and he now heard only an owl hooting.

There was a soft thickness to the woods that absorbed sound like a plush carpet, muffling it and keeping in the heat of the forest gathered during the day. The scent of dried decaying pine needles was heavy in the air, the smell of fall that reminded Landon of the leaf piles he and Damien used to rake up only to jump into and obliterate. They would throw masses of leaves at each other and bury each other in leaves and needles, and then rake a path through the leaves on the lawn, creating different imaginary chambers and rooms and vaults. They would invite other kids to play tag within their structure, the only rule being to stay within the confines of its walls and not reach over the walls of the maze, which were treated as real walls from the ground to the sky. He remembered swinging on the swing set in their backyard and jumping into the piles of leaves as a cushion. There was never the slightest care about bugs and ticks and dirt; the only consideration was how much fun could be had.

28

Chester roamed under the moonlight, delirious with hunger and thirst. He knew he could survive if he wanted to, but he didn't *want to* anymore. He wasn't sure why he had taken such great steps to continue his life in such a solitary and meaningless manner. What was the purpose of his life now? He served no function that he could see, other than to survive and experience the world every day. That used to be enough, to watch the sun rise and set and have no rules, no boundaries and no deadlines. In a way, it was beautiful and pure, but he knew he was kidding himself. It wasn't the life he was meant to live. Maybe it was the lack of food in his system. Maybe he was becoming malnourished. Maybe this was nature's way of telling him that his life had run its course, and it was time to give in to fate and return his body to the Earth.

He could have died in prison, and it would have ended there. He could have been killed any day when he drove to work before that.

He thought about Emily and the look on her face when she threatened him. Then there was the scared look afterward, the look of a frightened little girl who knew she had gone too far. It wasn't her fault. She had no sense of consequences. She had lived a privileged life and had not yet learned. He would be the ultimate lesson for her, assuming she was alive. He prayed that she would be found alive and well and could return to her family.

The moon was full on such a clear night, and he could see all the craters in it as he lay down. A slight smile formed across his lips at the image of the Energizer Bunny that could be seen in the full moon, as pointed out to him by his ex-fiancé.

He took a deep breath of the cool, crisp night air that reeked of the changing of seasons, of a harsh winter to come, freezing weather and snowstorms. He let his head slowly recline and clunk back on the cold, hard metal of the train rail as if it were a soft pillow. It wouldn't be long now.

29

Landon heard the train horn sound in the distance. He saw a flash of her face in his mind, the terror, her mouth wide open with nothing coming out. She was trying to call out to him to find her. The horn blew again, sending chills down his spine and making him freeze, staring into the night. He remembered putting the coins on the rails with her. He remembered the time they all got a little too close, and the train blasted the air horn right as it passed them, leaving them all without hearing for a minute.

The train horn howled through the night like a banshee tearing through the forest where no one goes, wailing its way through fields and empty hollows. He had to go to the train.

Landon remembered the model trains, playing with her. He could still see the smile on her face as she cranked her throttle all the way up in sick anticipation of the impending collision. The train horn sounded, and he could see their two trains coming together on a crash course toward a disaster that no one could stop. *Oh God*, he thought, *Oh God...they shouldn't have gone there; they shouldn't have gone to the train....*

He heard the crunches in the forest behind him. He was so frightened by everything that he began to run. He didn't care who or what was trying to scare him—he was going to find out the truth tonight, no matter what it entailed.

He remembered their feet walking the same ground he stomped across now, seeing the same stump that their two flashlights had illuminated on Halloween night. He heard the train in the distance rumbling past like thunder, with shrill haunting squeals from heavy metal wheels under boxcars.

I'm coming for you, Emily.

He remembered her telling him to keep his costume on when they snuck out of their houses and met. When he asked her why, she told him because it was still Halloween, and it was the one time each year when they could pretend to be someone else and forget all their problems.

The two of them had headed out into the darkness together with such careless vigor, such excitement; he didn't know where they were heading or why they were going there, but he knew he was with her and, without a doubt, that there was nothing he would rather be doing in the world.

"Come on," she yelled to him excitedly, seeming to make a game of how quickly they could get to wherever they were going.

"Why are we running?" he yelled after her, not really caring about the answer.

"Because we can!" she responded with delight.

It was almost as if they were running to relieve the awkwardness of holding hands, to make it seem acceptable.

"Where are we going?" he asked her between labored breaths.

"You'll see."

They ran out into a clearing together, hand in hand. At first, he had no idea where they were, having become totally disoriented in the dark, but then he regained his bearings. He was out by the rail tracks, in the clearing, near the place where they used to flatten the coins on the tracks.

"Out there," she said to him excitedly, pointing somewhere in the dark down the line of the tracks.

Having no idea what she was talking about, he ran with her again, laughing as he tripped and nearly sent them both tumbling to the ground. She laughed as well as she dragged him along, the two of them racing toward nothing in particular.

Then his tone changed. He slowed his pace, realizing what she was dragging him toward, and gave a great deal of resistance, slowing her down as well, nearly making her lose her grip on his hand, which she then tightened her hold on. "We're heading toward the bridge," he said with a certain amount of distress in his voice, although he was still having fun. "The bridge is right up here. We need to stop."

"Why? Are you afraid?" she asked tauntingly.

"No.... That's just not a good idea, especially in the dark. Are you crazy?"

"Maybe. I don't know," she said with a careless shrug and a giggle. "Maybe you're driving me crazy."

"I think you're driving *me* crazy," he mused, pulling her back toward him.

She giggled some more as she dragged him toward the bridge, and they engaged in a playful tug of war, nearly pulling each other to the ground.

"Come on," she insisted. "I've never been out there before."

"That's insane," Landon argued. "It's like two-hundred feet down."

"I know! Isn't it awesome?"

"You're out of your mind."

"Come out with me," she tempted him.

"No," he said, a little more defiantly now. "No way."

"Come on," she insisted, trying to persuade him. "Please?" she bounced a little on her toes, making her ponytail hop.

It made him surprisingly weak. It was the first time he realized that if a pretty girl looked at him a certain way and acted a certain way, he was powerless to her. He looked at the bridge extending into the darkness, so far out. "All right," he gave in, feeling ashamed for caving but feeling free and wonderful at the same time, "but just a little ways out."

"I want to go all the way to the middle," she insisted in an upbeat tone. "I've always wanted to be out there in the middle, at its highest point."

"But what if a train comes?" he blurted out, clearly revealing his fear now.

"A train won't come. One came through, just like, fifteen minutes ago. Another won't come through here for at least an hour. I used to time them. Don't worry."

Landon was not convinced and stood silent, looking at her longingly.

"Don't worry so much," she calmed him. "Even if a train did come, which it's *not* going to, all you have to do is lay down along the side of the bridge and it will go right over you."

He scoffed at her reasoning. "You've tried this before?"

"No, but I know it will work," she said confidently. "I'll tell you what. I'll sweeten the deal for you," she said with a nice smile. "If you make it out to the middle with me, I'll let you kiss me."

He looked her in the eyes, stunned she had just said that. The way she looked at him, puckered her lips and then pouted a little at him, it was hopeless. All common sense and good judgment went straight out the window. He was lost.

"Just walk in the middle down the tracks," she said to him as they teetered on opposite rails, holding hands to help balance each other as they walked foot over foot in a straight line down the rails like two tightrope walkers in a circus. "The sides can be a little sketchy."

"What does that mean?" Landon looked over at her sharply.

"I mean they might be missing a piece here and there, or there are holes in places, just that sort of thing."

"Holes in places? Great," he said sarcastically and laughed to himself, not quite sure if she was joking or not. He was so focused on balancing on the rail and holding her hand and how much fun he was having that he entirely forgot that they were on a live railroad bridge, and a train could come at any moment, regardless of what she said.

"Right here," she said suddenly, seeming surprised. "We made it! We're in the middle! See? We're still alive."

"At the moment," he mused.

"And I think I promised you something," she said, grabbing a hold of his other hand, pulling him off the rail and bringing him close; her standing on her rail made them equal in height as he stood in the middle of the track. The excitement of being out there where they shouldn't be, the most dangerous place she could think of, the cool night air on Halloween night, the moon lighting up the clouds in the sky, painting the night sky a range of grays and blacks, it was all so magical, so spiritual, so fun, so *grown up*. She pulled him closer and leaned in herself until they pressed their lips together.

Her lips were soft and so thin, and she smelled like flowers up close. He had finally experienced what everyone had always been talking about, what he had seen in the movies and on TV a hundred times, but to experience it for himself could never be compared or described. Much to his delight, after they had held their lips together for a moment, she didn't pull back right away, although he was prepared to, unsure of what to do. She pressed her lips harder against his and moved even closer to him, jumping off her rail and standing face-to-face with him, looking up at him slightly, into his eyes. After she pulled her lips back very gently, she smiled at him softly, sweetly, exposing a different side of the tomboy he had come to know. There was something so feminine, delicate and tender about her, and it marveled him how different girls were from boys.

Then her face went pale. Her eyes moved past him.

There was suddenly something very wrong about her expression. There was a brief inhalation, a shallow gasp that was not released. Her body went rigid; her eyes became wide, her pupils stones; her mouth hung loosely open, as though she was receiving an electric jolt that had captured her and frozen her in time. He would never forget the pure terror in her stone eyes.

Before he could ask her what was wrong, before the words could even form on his lips and before he could think of the words to say, he was turning to his right, swiveling, alarmed and instantly panicked, to follow her terror-stricken stare behind him. He turned his body halfway around just in time to see the blow coming, a blur of movement, a large figure looming over him, towering over him in the darkness. Landon flinched, cowered and threw his arms up as high as they could, which was not high enough to block the attack that came. A heavy impact rocked his skull and sent his upper teeth slamming against his lower teeth with a crack that was especially loud within his skull. He spun in the darkness and landed harshly across the railroad tracks, the cold steel of the left train rail crushing his lower back upon impact.

A shrill scream erupted from Emily that pierced into the darkness of the gorge below.

Heavy footsteps shuffled through the gravel and dirt between the railroad ties, and Landon felt himself grabbed by the collar. He was still disoriented and dazed. The attack had come so quickly that he didn't know what was happening, why it was happening or what direction he was facing.

Landon found himself hoisted in the air, whisked off the railroad tracks by a force so powerful that he was putty in its grasp before he could think of fighting it or trying to free himself. A grunt was forced from him as the wind was knocked out of him again. He found himself dangling upside down over the side of the bridge with infinite darkness below.

"How dare you put my daughter's life in danger!" the man hollered at Landon. "Is this your idea of a good time? Coming out here to the middle of a train bridge at night, when she's supposed to be safe in her home with her parents?"

"Daddy! No!" Emily cried at the figure, rushing up and reaching around him trying to grab onto Landon's arms.

"You think it's fun to take my daughter's life into your own hands? How does this feel? How does it feel having your life in *my* hands? How about I let go of you right now?"

"Daddy, please, stop!" Emily pleaded with him.

"I'm going to drop you off this bridge like the trash you are.... You and your worthless parents, your worthless poor family, working at my mill like slaves their entire life...you should all be dropped right off this bridge, you worthless, useless, meaningless paper dolls...."

"No! He's going to fall! Please, Dad!" she screamed at him as she saw his arms shaking with such fury they seemed they might let go, throwing him forcefully down into the ravine. Fearing for Landon's life, she threw herself at the two of them with her arms extending through his outstretched arms out over the bridge rail, grabbing Landon's other hand.

Her father roared with rage at her act of defiance and compassion for such a hooligan, and with much more strength than intended, he flung her away with his free hand.

He had meant only to brush her off, but instead sent her hurling wildly backward. Emily's arms flailed as she rolled through the air with the flowing silk of her genie costume sailing around her. When she landed, she hit only briefly before suddenly disappearing from view. There was a brief loud scream that instantly became muffled and trailed down into the abyss below, moving further away from them both, into the darkness beneath. Then the scream abruptly stopped.

Landon remembered the thud of her hitting the ground on that otherwise soundless night. It was an unmistakable solid thump from the bottom of the ravine that instantly destroyed any hope in either of their hearts that she would somehow survive the fall.

Landon found himself hurled through the air—he thought he was being thrown off the bridge, into the dark after her, but instead landed harshly on the edge of the bridge within its rail, falling back against it.

There was silence for a moment. Her father darted to the edge of the bridge and desperately peered over it, his hands placed wide on the railing. There was not another sound. The silence was horrifying, watching this man, knowing what had just happened that they both refused to believe.

It had happened so quickly. There was a moment of confusion, a loss of bearings, and time had stopped. She wasn't on the bridge anymore. There were no second chances; there was no getting her back. In that split second, the moment she had left the bridge, she was gone forever.

Mr. Rose wailed out crazed cries into the night like a madman. His elbows raised, and he yanked at his hair, tearing out fistfuls with both fists clenched and shaking. His arms shook violently, trembling, as he cried out one long, horrible moan into the night air.

Landon slumped against the bridge's railing. His arms extended out in midair with palms open and fingers spread as if to catch her as she fell.

After what seemed like an eternity of shock and confusion, stammering, stuttering, screaming and crying, Mr. Rose's focus suddenly landed on Landon. Landon could remember Mr. Rose's face looking down at him, propped up against the side of the bridge with his hands still in the air.

"*You killed her*," he said intensely, insanely, almost under his breath.

Landon tried to push himself back, but only managed to shift himself up a little. He had nowhere to go and was too scared to move.

"*You killed my Emily.*" The words came with rage so deep it made him tremble.

Landon tried to shake his head. He tried to tell him that it was *her* idea, that he would never have harmed Emily, but it didn't matter now. He remembered the feeling of Mr. Rose suddenly lunging at him and attacking him, when he had nowhere to run. Landon cowered with his hands up to cover his face and pulled his knees forward against his body into a fetal position, his only defense, as the onslaught came. He remembered the big powerful fingers that squeezed his throat so tightly he couldn't breathe, the hands that then pulled him forward by the throat and thrust his head back violently, smashing it into the rusty rail of the bridge—and then again, and again.

Then he remembered the thunder, the squealing of metal on metal and feeling the vibrations and sound waves through his battered body, echoing through his pounding head. He was baffled by the darkness over him. He had awoken with a total loss of bearings and no idea what had happened. He realized there were train cars thundering right over his head, just feet away from him. The wind it created was so powerful that he was afraid it would blow him off the bridge. The deafening roar seemed to last forever, but then it stopped as suddenly as it had begun. He was alone in the dark. He didn't know where he was or why, but he knew he had to run as far away as he could.

30

It was no longer Halloween night. Landon found himself back in reality, returned from the haunting night that had traumatized him, in the exact spot where his terrifying memory had ended. He was alone again, in the middle of the bridge in the dark, where he had been left for dead Halloween night. Emily was gone, but it felt like she had just fallen. He wanted to help her, to run down and save her, but he knew in his heart that there was no way she could have survived her fall.

The sound of the train that night was like a thunderstorm, making the vibrations on the bridge under his feet shoot straight through his stomach and into his spine. The sounds from his nightmare still lingered, over a week later, despite having returned to reality. The tears still formed in his eyes, his nose began running and a chill ran through to his soul that made him clench himself and shake. Despite his return to reality, the rumbling of the train persisted, refusing to fade with his memory.

Suddenly, it occurred to him that the sound was growing in strength at an alarming rate.

Landon jumped up from his crouched position on the side of the bridge and sprang to his feet. There was an intense light in the distance, far down on the section of tracks before the bridge began, and it was approaching quickly. It was a round bright white light that made his eyes squint, even at its great distance. Landon stood stunned for a moment, unsure of what to do, refusing to accept the immediate peril he suddenly found himself in before realizing that he needed to move; he needed to run for his life. The side of the bridge was peppered with holes and missing portions, making it a treacherous walk in the dark. He swiveled around sharply to run back, down the center of the tracks between the two rails that he and Emily had used that night to balance themselves on, but as soon as he turned and sprang forward, away from the light coming at him, he slammed into a solid object in his path.

He felt something grab onto him and hold him tightly, preventing him from running—it was a set of large arms holding him hostage. He was unable to fight the strength of the arms wrapped around him and couldn't run off the bridge. He yelled, both in fear of the man who had grabbed him and the train fast approaching behind him, as he threw himself wildly against the man's grasp and wriggled and squirmed, but the man held a firm and confident grasp on him, steady and still.

"*You should have died that night, too,*" Mr. Rose said down to him in a low, grave tone.

Landon was horrified to face her father again, on the bridge with him just as he had been that night.

"*It should have been you!*" Mr. Rose cried out, squeezing him harder. "*Not her!*"

He held Landon in the middle of the tracks, between the two rails. Facing the white light approaching, Landon could see it had entered the bridge and was coming at them at an unstoppable speed.

"*Do you know what it's like?*" Mr. Rose said down to Landon, crying, in a strange, agonized tone, "*to bury your own daughter?*"

The train horn blared madly at them to get out of the way. The engineer had finally spotted the large man holding the young boy captive in the center of the tracks, awaiting the inevitable.

"*Do you know what it's like to carry her broken body away?*" Mr. Rose yelled over the train's horn and approaching thunder.

The horn howled non-stop. The engineer desperately attempted to warn them against what he saw coming.

"*Do you know what it's like to live with yourself, knowing that you did it to her? How can you go on after that? How do you live with yourself? Tell me!*" he screamed in Landon's ear, which he held so close his lips touched it. "*You tell me!*"

Landon could feel the train horn blasting through him like the brass section in a band, the sound waves tearing through him, as the approaching unstoppable murderous mass of steel hurled toward them and would surely reduce them both to pulp on the tracks.

Landon closed his eyes. He held his breath, preparing for the impact. He then felt a hard kiss on the back of his head through his hair.

Landon suddenly found himself flying through the air with great force, rolling end over end, and then slamming into the ground. He hit the hard solid surface roughly and was pinned on the ground. He was certain he had been hit by the train and didn't understand how he hadn't been torn apart. The train roared past him with such thunder and force that it made him throw his arms up over his head and flatten himself out on the ground for fear of being hit or sucked under the passing freight cars. He realized he hadn't been hit. Her father had thrown him out of the way at the last second. He didn't know why. He only knew that he was alive, he had chosen to save him at the last second; perhaps he couldn't bear the thought of being responsible for ending another child's life. Maybe he couldn't intentionally hurt someone else, especially the only other person so close to his daughter, and at the last moment, he realized it wouldn't bring her back, that Landon wasn't to blame and didn't deserve to die.

As the train cars passed by, he cowered, fearing they would somehow hit him, seeming mere inches from his head. The train's wheels screeched horribly into the night as the massive freight train attempted to slow the long line of freight cars behind it, rumbling overhead with no signs of stopping soon. The brakes of the locomotive were getting farther away but the freight cars still rumbled overhead like a tornado ready to suck him up into those heavy steel wheels that passed inches away like giant pizza cutters on the track, with hundreds more behind them, leaving no chance for escape or survival. As he hugged the floor of the bridge, he became aware that he was not alone—a pair of hands was pinning him to the bridge, protecting him.

Finally, the last car passed overhead, and there was an instant silence, at least compared to the horrific sound that had consumed him. The air was still, the wind stopped and nothing was sucking him upward anymore.

He felt himself being released by the strong grasp that had saved his life. He twisted his neck to look back up over his shoulder, pushing himself up off the dirt and metal of the bridge to twist his body around to see.

He saw a man backing away from him in slow motion, looking down at him stunned, unable to comprehend what had just happened. He was a man of average height and dressed with dark colored, plain, loose baggy clothing. As Landon's eyes focused, he could see the long beard in the moonlight. He knew it was Chester.

Landon realized that her father had been hit by the train. There was no body present though, and as far as he could tell in the dark, there was no blood.

Chester took another step back, still in disbelief, perhaps wondering how he had managed to save the boy on the tracks or amazed at how close he had just come to being killed himself by the train. He turned, tripping a little on the tracks, and swiftly took a few steps away, heading toward the end of the bridge, back to solid ground, leaving Landon there, alone but alive.

"Wait," Landon called after him, holding up a hand and reaching out to stop him.

Chester turned around to look back at Landon on the ground. He stopped moving away, seeming concerned that he may have been hurt.

"I know it wasn't you," Landon stated to him, reaching a hand out to him in the dark as if to grab onto him and keep him from disappearing again. "I know you didn't do anything to Emily," Landon continued.

"So, you know," Chester said with a hopeless shrug. "I've known that since it happened. It doesn't change a thing." His figure turned in the dark, and he started away again, down the tracks, back into the night.

"But I might have proof," Landon called after him from the floor of the bridge, feeling the sharp little rocks digging into the soft flesh of his palms. "I can get her diary," he proclaimed proudly with great hope. "She talks all about what happened and how her father knew. She admits that she made the whole thing up. And my friend Damien knew too. Emily swore him to secrecy, but he knows that you never did anything to her."

Chester seemed unaffected by this news. After all he had been through, the words meant very little to him. He knew that those who had turned on him would never forgive him. "That's real big of you, kid," he said to Landon kindly, in the most positive and caring tone he could muster. "The damage is done, though, I'm afraid. My life has already been damaged beyond repair."

"We can fix it," Landon said with newfound joy and hope, although still very much shaken. "It's not too late."

31

It had been a long and tiring hike into the forest on a sunny afternoon to a spot so beautiful and perfect that Landon knew instantly it was her final resting place. Carter had gone with him to show him the way, but had barely said a word the entire journey. He stood in his black overcoat with his hands in his pockets, silently staring down at the ground with Landon at his side.

In a small clearing of evergreen trees overlooking the valley below arose a small mound elevated slightly above the ground around it. The fresh dirt that covered it was darker in color that the surrounding earth, with rocks placed around the edge of the grave to line its border. At the head of the mound stood a small wooden cross carved from what looked like antique wood, which stood about a foot tall. Landon wondered if it had been taken from the Rose's lavish home since he had seen similar wood in the library and Emily's room.

It had been decided by the town and the police force that they would not move the body, but rather, let her remain in the setting her father chose as her final resting place.

Landon knew now that she had done so much wrong during her time in this world, despite the good she brought to it. She had been willing to destroy Chester's life for selfish reasons. He thought about how she had hurt Chester so badly, and it made him bitter, causing him to question his entire friendship with her. He had held her on such a high pedestal, as did her father and most of the townspeople, but he quickly realized that she was young and made a mistake that she regretted deeply.

He would always remember the magical times they shared together. She wasn't a monster; she was his greatest friend, the girl he had quickly come to know and trust and did everything with. She was the first girl he had ever kissed when they were together on the bridge that night—and that beautiful memory now blended with the nightmare that ensued. He knew that the town would never be the same again after this tragedy. The locals had held out hope that somehow she was still out there, that she would be miraculously found alive, perhaps only injured, and joyous to be rescued and return home to a life of blissful luxury and privilege, but that day would never come.

Landon thought about her father and the torture he must have endured, and why he felt he had to bury her out there and had to hide her away. It was the guilt, Landon figured, that consumed him, the knowledge that his own actions and obsession killed her. He was not in the right frame of mind after he lost his daughter, and he panicked and did his best to hide what he had done. Landon couldn't imagine her father finding her body at the bottom of the gorge below the train bridge, then taking her broken body into his arms to carry her. Landon thought about how long he must have walked with her body, looking for the best place to bury her in the forest, and it nearly brought him to tears. No matter what sort of person he was and what he had done, no father deserves to live that nightmare. Once she was there in the resting place he had chosen, it must have tortured him that his daughter would not get a proper burial and her loved ones would not be able to pay their respects, but he was too afraid of what he would face. The damage was done at that point, and he did what he felt he must.

Based on a tip from one of the local police officers, Carter was able to track down Winston in the Gibson State

Prison, located the next town over. He had been arrested for possession of marijuana after Mr. Rose phoned the local police, despite Winston's claim that he had stopped smoking and carrying it after Mr. Rose spoke to him over a year earlier. Winston was surprisingly relieved to see Carter and was anxious to share his story. He told Carter that Mr. Rose had him arrested by the sheriff shortly after Carter saw him pulling the wagon into the forest. Winston's cousin had befriended Chester while he was in prison, and he had been helping Chester survive in the woods by bringing leftovers, expired foods and supplies from the mansion out to him with the wagon. Winston knew that Chester had been wrongfully accused and imprisoned for a crime he didn't commit. He also felt horribly guilty that he knew this all along and never did anything to stop it, for fear of losing his job—or worse.

After the truck hit Carter's car, Sheriff Reynolds told Mr. Rose instantly about the strange actions of his butler. Mr. Rose followed Winston into the forest the next time he went, suspecting what he was doing, and learned the location of Chester's home. Mr. Rose had forgotten about Chester once the fiasco that Emily created was over. He had assumed that Chester was long-gone, moved to a different town or still in prison. He was shocked to learn that Chester was living in the woods surrounding Victory Falls, not only free but so dangerously close to the town that had rejected him. Mr. Rose knew it was best to eliminate the problem, just as he had eliminated Winston from the picture. A ghost from his past had resurfaced, and he was already not in the right frame of mind to handle it properly. So, just past midnight on Thursday, he trekked to the old mill and set it on fire, hoping Chester wouldn't make it out alive.

Winston knew all along that something was wrong with Mr. Rose. His boss had been acting very unusual, very strained and stressed, which at first he thought was due solely to the disappearance of his daughter. He became very uneasy about Mr. Rose's mysterious journeys outside the house until one or two in the morning. Winston had assumed he was out searching endlessly for Emily, but Mr. Rose only left the house at night and always appeared heavily intoxicated when he returned. What Winston hadn't realized at the time was that when Mr. Rose left the house, he had been stalking Landon, fearful that he would remember the events of that fateful night. It was Mr. Rose standing on the front lawn of the Daniels' home that night, perhaps trying to lure Landon out—or find a way in—so that Landon, too, could be eradicated.

Winston knew the truth about Emily and Chester. As much as he tried to mind his own business, it was almost impossible not to overhear conversations in such a quiet house where every little noise echoed. People like Mr. Rose grow so accustomed to servants, cooks and maids around them all the time that they forget that their employees are people, with minds of their own, who can hear and remember things said. Those who worked for him were not mere paper dolls.

Mr. Rose's remains had been spread over a quarter mile by the train before it finally came to a stop. A closed-casket service was held, but it was sparsely attended. Those who showed up to pay their respects were almost exclusively family members who felt obligated to make an appearance.

With Carter's help, Landon was able to enter the backyard and retrieve Emily's diary from her life-sized dollhouse. Just as Damien had claimed, she had written extensively about how she had wrongfully accused Chester of molesting her. She had been tortured by guilt and remorse not only for creating such a nightmare for Chester, but for not being able to stop what she had started. She had wanted to come clean with the school board and confess that she had fabricated the story, but her father wouldn't allow it. She had told Mr. Rose the truth, and he chose to proceed with pressing charges against Chester Thompson and sending him to prison. Mr. Rose would sooner see Chester rot in prison than admit to the community that his daughter told such a disgusting lie, to risk ruining the family name. Now, the Rose mansion stood empty on Main Street, a gaudy monstrosity that represented only loneliness and heartache.

The media had a field day with how Chester was wrongfully accused and he was swarmed with reporters requesting interviews. The diary and Winston's testimony brought an undeniable truth to the incident.

Chester tried to get in touch with his ex-fiancé to share the great news, but she didn't return his calls. Although he knew he could never have him back, at the very least, he wanted to see his dog, Chip, again. In the back of his mind, he believed that if he could at least visit the dog and be around his ex-fiancé again, if only for a brief period, he could rekindle what they once shared, but the call back never came. He had been left behind, a piece of her past that she had removed from her life like a cancer—just like his family had, just like his friends had.

Chester grieved for three days exactly. He sulked and buried himself in the comfort of the grief he had felt over the last two years of his life. Giving up was so much easier than trying, especially when you have a reasonable excuse for giving up. At the end of the third day, watching the sunset, he stopped grieving and realized the opportunity he had been given. He had been granted a new beginning and felt blessed that something positive had come from such an awful tragedy, all the heartache, and the two prison sentences he served—one in prison and the other in solitary isolation.

His record had been cleared. He was free to reestablish himself and rebuild his life. He would meet someone else someday, someone better. He would get another dog. Life was beginning again for him, though it was sadly over for Emily and her father. Chester wasn't angry at them for what they had done. He needed to leave the bitterness behind him, and he certainly felt deep sorrow for the horrible fate they met.

All that mattered was where he could go from here and what he could do. He had his entire life ahead of him and he knew, as he skipped down the steps of the county courthouse, that the eleven-year-old boy, Landon Daniels, had saved his life as much as he had saved Landon's on the tracks that night.

When a mysterious figure appears in the psychiatric ward of the local hospital, a young nurse realizes this man possesses extraordinary abilities that leave her stunned—and doing anything she can to help him. Tortured by his inability to end his own life, the man is forced to face his strange connection to a series of bizarre murders. Homicide investigator Carter VanDusen races against time to learn the truth...but fate has something much greater in store for everyone involved.

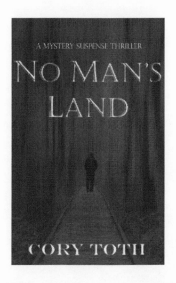

Hunter Fairchild fled his hometown of Madison twenty years ago and vowed never to return. An accomplished surgeon, he has repressed bitter memories of his childhood and buried them far beneath his beautiful home, his fancy cars and his gorgeous wife, who can't be pleased. However, when the small town of Madison is plagued by an unknown horror that dwells in the surrounding forest, he is mysteriously drawn back and forced to face the truth.

Hunter and three unlikely friends from his past reunite to embark on a journey that will bring their greatest fears to light. As flashbacks of Hunter's childhood unite with the present adventure, the group must track down the menace and lay it to rest...but first they must confront the beast within each one of them.

Calvin Strong had everything in the world going for him. Then,
after a business misfortune and a stormy relationship, he lost
everything but his sanity and his love for his baby daughter. He
is now struggling to make it through each day, emotionally and
financially, when disaster strikes and the floodgates of Hell are
opened. Danger lurks in the background, tearing at the fabric of
his fragile existence. Someone has been watching him. Someone
is following his every move, waiting in the shadows, terrorizing
him with unknown motives. He begins to suspect everyone in
his life, including himself. He must fight to learn what is
happening before it is too late for him…and his family.

Cory Toth is the author of four novels: *Firefly*, *Paper Dolls*, *Ashes to Ashes*, and *No Man's Land*. Toth was born and raised in Upstate New York and draws inspiration for his novels from local towns and landscapes. When he is not writing, he spends much of his free time helping the American Red Cross.